WINGS OF LIFE

THE LAST PHOENIX: BOOK FIVE

STEPHANIE MIRRO

TANNHAUSER PRESS

ALSO BY STEPHANIE MIRRO

THE LAST PHOENIX
Wings of Fire
Wings of Death
Wings of Winter
Wings of Magic
Wings of Life
Wings of Deceit
Wings of Mercy

IMMORTAL RELICS
Curse of the Vampire
Fury of the Gods
Revenge of the Witch
Rise of the Demons

COLLECTIONS
The Outsiders: An Hourlings Anthology

Dedication

For Rachel Green, your enthusiastic and laugh-out-loud feedback has kept me confident that I'm on the right track with V and her shenanigans. Thank you for sticking with me through this series.

AUTHOR'S NOTE

Dear Reader,

If you're a fan of spicy scenes, go forth and prosper.

If you're not, you can skip over chapters 6 and 27 without missing out on the rest of the story. But after 4 books, Veronica needed her Big Bang.

Mom and Dad,

Skip chapters 6 and 27, or just lie to me and say you skipped them. Please and thank you.

CHAPTER 1

Friday Afternoon

Time had never felt so ominous before, like it was slowly but surely sucking the life out of me. Only a few days had passed since my coronation as tsarina, but too much time had passed since I stumbled my way out of that godsdamn portal.

I needed to get back to the human world. Back home to Miami.

Back to *Thane*.

I tapped the arm of the throne in an impatient cadence, my nerves not allowing me to be still.

Not just any throne, either—*my* throne. What a ridiculous thought. I was the farthest thing from a queen or even a good leader. I was a thief, for flame's sake. A reformed thief, but still not exactly high on the morality scale.

Becoming royalty had never interested me, and leading certainly wasn't my forte. I was self-aware enough to admit that I was way too selfish. Supposedly that self-awareness made me a better ruler.

According to Pietr, anyway.

Sure, I'd been able to fool everyone for a short time, pretending I'd accepted my role as a queen of a world I'd never even heard of until very recently. But pretending had been easy when rage and grief consumed me after losing Pavel and finding out Galina was responsible for my little brother's death.

Now, we were back to normal, everyday Veronica Neill, and I was bored as fuck.

My throne sat to one side of the circular rotunda, columns holding up the massive, domed ceiling. Everything in here, from the floor to the ceiling, glittered with the sparkling reddish-gold hue of fireglass. The unique building material made from sand and phoenix fire was malleable when first heated, but as strong as steel once cooled.

The rotunda was also the room where Pavel had died. To this day, I couldn't enter it without glancing at the spot on the floor where he'd fallen, wishing each time that I had dealt with William, that godsdamned fae necromancer, earlier. Even if it meant never finding my way to Mirfeniksa, at least my friend would still be alive. I was sure the rebels would have brought Galina down eventually.

My gaze found its way there now, my shoulders sagging under the memory of his final words. A fresh wave of grief crashed over me.

"Find your mate," Pavel had said, and I wouldn't rest until I did just that.

From her usual place to the right of my throne, Lena bent down toward my ear, the beads in her black dreadlocks clinking together. She whispered, "Your tapping is driving me crazy."

With great effort, I held in the snort that wanted to escape and shot her a side glare. Light blue eyes twinkled with her amusement. She knew I had to pretend like I was listening to the dignitary complaining in front of me. If anyone was going crazy, it was most definitely me. She could tune out the whining at least.

Unfortunately, snorting would offend the dignitary. Not that I *really* cared what he thought. He had become a rich man under Galina's rule and was complaining now about the injustice of the reform I brought to Mirfeniksa. Injustice as in requiring him to obey the laws that had existed for millennia before her awful rule. I would have put him in his place an hour ago, except the last thing I needed right now was a new enemy to deal with.

I eyed the phoenix droning on, the last one I'd have to see today. Like most male phoenixes, his coloring was bright and eye-catching—mostly blond hair, turquoise irises, and an olive hue to his skin, similar to Lena's. His immaculate clothing and unmarked skin told me he'd been born into a wealthy family, likely never knowing a hard day's work in his life. I doubted he'd even fought in the battle of Sokol.

Yet here he was, whining about the people who poured their blood, sweat, and tears into his land like *they* were the problem. I ground my teeth together.

Time to put an end to this bullshit, new enemy or not.

"I've heard enough," I announced, cutting him off. "You will abide by the laws or forfeit your lands to me. You may go."

I sounded so regal these days you would think I'd been practicing since birth. No, this was just pure exhaustion and anxiety talking. I stood and strode from the room, Lena's snickers following close on my heels as the dignitary's splutters faded away.

"And to think," she said when we were alone, resting one hand casually on her sword's pommel, "you said you weren't cut out to be a tsarina."

This time, I let out a snort. "I'm not. I just can't handle these entitled assholes thinking I owe them something. Shouldn't they be the ones owing *me* because they let that deranged *uzurpator* take over?"

There I went with my royal wisdom again. But hey, at least I was remembering more Yazyk. My lessons in the phoenix language were painful for everyone involved.

Lena chuckled but didn't respond, knowing me well enough now not to encourage my outbursts in public.

She had been a true gift from the gods these past few days. She and her twin sister, Liz, had become my close friends in the short amount of time I'd been here, but it was Lena's mastery of resting bitch face and her colorful vocabulary that kept the vultures at bay.

Not to mention her skill in the battle at Sokol had made her a legend. Other soldiers and guards spoke of the warrior woman in awe. I wished I'd had the chance to see her fighting in action. Maybe someday. With my track record, I was sure to make a new enemy before too long.

Open windows provided plenty of light and fresh air as we strode down the hallway. Falcons of all sizes and colors swooped past in the distance, popping out of or disappearing into the blue-green leaves surrounding us. Only the palace guards who flew in human form could get closer to the bird's nest palace.

Nestled among the branches of a colossal tree, the palace overlooked Sokol, the capital of Mirfeniksa. It was a good thing my kind wasn't afraid of heights because the tree and city sat atop a high plateau, where canals and rivers crisscrossed across the hilltop. Crystal-blue water flowed beneath massive roots and carved its way through the fireglass city like streets. At the plateau's edges, waterfalls cascaded to the valley floor below.

The view always took my breath away.

We passed a group of phoenixes in servant's clothing who dropped their gazes and bowed as I neared. Only a few more doors to go until I could breathe comfortably again, without eyes on me or people bowing everywhere I went.

The hallway leading to my personal quarters was way too long to be convenient or practical, but I refused to use the same rooms Galina had. Whether it was rational or not, I didn't want to think of her every time I entered my room. I'd rather turn it into a griffin roost and let them shit all over the place.

Galina.

My lip curled involuntarily. Using some sort of never-before-seen sorcery, that despicable woman had convinced my people that my mother was barren. She claimed it was a sign from the gods that my bloodline's millennia-long rule had ended.

She wasn't even a phoenix herself, a fact she'd somehow hidden from everyone. I had yet to figure out what the hell she was.

I scratched at the tingling red mark above my left boob—a phoenix bonding mark. The spot had itched incessantly since last night, a fact I was sure wasn't a good sign and only added to my overall anxiety. Because of course my inner flame just had to go and fall for a grim reaper destined for angel wings.

"You'll be there soon," Lena said, eyeing my scratching. Our footsteps echoed in the now-empty hall. "One last dinner, and then you're free to go."

I rolled my eyes as we neared the last door. "Free for a day or two at best. Then it's back to figuring out how I can pass the crown over to Pietr so I can be free for real."

As we approached my room, she nodded to the guard posted outside.

Vladimir had been one of Galina's bodyguards, held under her spell for almost thirty years. Whatever supernatural type Galina had been, she'd figured out a way to siphon phoenix magic and blend it with dark shadow magic that she used to control Sokol's inhabitants.

Her unique blend of magic was vaguely familiar, but I couldn't put a finger on it.

Once she died and Vladimir had come to, he'd pledged to redeem himself. He had proven resourceful and loyal, never once giving me a reason to distrust him.

He bowed deeply and opened the door. "Your majesty."

I smiled. "Thank you, Vladimir."

"You do realize we're a matriarchal society, right?" Lena asked and went through the door first, checking for any intruders. "You can't just pass the crown over to Pietr."

"So you all keep telling me." I followed her in and waited for the door to close again.

As soon as it clicked shut, I let my cape fall to the ground and collapsed on the bed, arms and legs spread wide. I'd made sure all my royal dresses allowed for a wide range of movement. I just hadn't thought it would be for flopping onto beds. "Do you want the job?"

"Not in a million years," she said, laughter tinting her voice.

"Okay, well, who says we can't become a best-leader-wins kind of society? You know Pietr would be so much better at all of this."

The mattress dipped as Lena sat beside me, though she was still poised and ready to spring into action should any threat present itself. "I mean, you're the rule-maker now. Do whatever you want. Just don't be surprised if you're the next one to catch a bullet between the eyes when the people blame you for the mess a man will make."

I gave a short, humorless laugh. She referred to the bullet that had lodged between Galina's eyes, courtesy of the little gift Pietr had given me before I faced her. Only one bullet remained in the historic six-shooter, and my aim had been too good to be true.

There was no doubt the gods had intervened.

Had I faced her at my full strength and not completely drained of magic from my fight with William, I wouldn't have had to kill her, just subdue her. That way, I could have asked her all the questions still rolling through my head—like what the hell she was—and *then* killed her.

Oh well. A bullet to the brain had done wonders for stopping the monster once and for all.

Pietr was nowhere near the monster that Galina had been. Like, on the opposite end of the good-versus-evil spectrum.

After our steamy, yet incredibly dissatisfying moment in the hot spring back in Haven, he'd been a perfect gentleman, treating me like nothing had happened—in a good way. He respected the bond I'd formed with Thane, and that was the end of it.

Fingers crossed, I'd be released from said bond once the reaper ascended to the angelic choir. Then maybe I could recreate that hot tub scene with a very happy and satisfying ending.

My eyes stung with sudden tears, and I pressed the heels of my hands into them.

Once I got over the heartbreak of losing Thane, anyway.

Regardless, there was no doubt in my mind that Pietr would make a fair and kind ruler. A better one than me.

If only I could convince everyone else of that fact.

CHAPTER 2

Friday Evening

I missed dinners in Haven's war room, deep in the cave that had sheltered us from the spellbound royal guards who'd flown overhead. Back before I was named tsarina and my world turned upside down.

Not that I wanted to sound ungrateful by mentioning it. I was beyond thankful for everything that had occurred since then. I'd found Maddox's killer and brought her to justice, freed this realm of a tyrant, and discovered the truth about my family.

Wins all around.

Except we'd lost Pavel, a loss that still made my heart clench at the most unexpected times, like when a random dimple appeared on someone's cheek.

The pain wasn't only from our physical losses, either. People ensnared by Galina's dark magic still struggled to let their guilt go, and it showed in their hollow gazes and furtive glances. They felt somehow responsible for her stealing the throne from my parents and forcing them to flee to the human world, but the phoenix realm never knew I existed until now.

They didn't know—or didn't want to *accept*—that her magic was almost too strong to resist, especially if they didn't see it coming.

Tonight, sitting at the head of a long-ass table that could easily seat thirty, under numerous jeweled fireglass chandeliers and surrounded by luxury few could fathom, dinner felt distant and cold, even with all my friends' laughter.

If I couldn't convince the phoenix population to accept Pietr as their leader, then I'd demand a smaller table in a cozy nook of the palace.

Lena slapped the fireglass table and roared with laughter. The sudden sound forced me back to the present once again.

I gazed at each of my friends' faces, taking in every detail. Losing Pavel had reminded me that our last moments together could come at any time. I didn't want to forget a single freckle or out-of-place hair.

Yelena and Lizabeta, better known as Lena and Liz, were identical in looks. They'd been blessed with bright blue eyes, olive skin, and jet-black hair, though Lena wore hers in dreadlocks while Liz wore braids.

They were not so alike in personality, however. Liz's

daily blue skirt identified her as a trained healer. More often than not, she'd displayed a calm and coolheaded demeanor, even amongst utter chaos.

In contrast, her sister's weapons and armor marked her as the fierce warrior that she was. Any chance I got, I teased Lena for being shorter than me. Getting away without getting hit had become a fun, challenging game.

Next to Liz sat Oleg with his dark red hair, green eyes, and the cutest freckles splattered across his brown face. His nickname, Egg, still cracked me up (no pun intended). He was a giant of a man, possibly due to actual giant genetics somewhere in his ancestry. He had a broad chest, thick neck, and muscles that would make a champion weightlifter weep.

Lines around his eyes and mouth showed he was older than the rest of the group here by a couple of centuries. His family had raised griffins, which explained the multitude of scars that crisscrossed the length of his bare arms.

I was pretty sure he and Liz would have mated marks by now, especially with how close they'd become since Pavel's death. Even tonight, they held hands beneath the table, something they would have never been caught doing back in the caves.

Across from them was Ivan, the young red-headed phoenix who reminded me so much of my brother Maddox, down to their shared emerald eye color. His realm walking ability had brought him to the human world and introduced me to the idea that I wasn't the last phoenix after all. Far from it, in fact.

Now, in a random turn of events, I was the leader of them all.

Between Ivan and me sat Pietr.

Oh, Pietr. The phoenix with the most mesmerizing rainbow-hued eyes, dark brown skin, and white-blond hair and beard. His deep, commanding voice still sent tingles down my spine. I had cracked his tough outer shell and found the gentle, kind man within.

If only I hadn't fallen in love with a grim reaper destined to leave me heartbroken, things might have turned out differently with Pietr. Maybe they still would, but I couldn't hope for anything past getting back to Thane in time to say goodbye.

My gaze drifted to the open seat where Pavel would have sat. He'd had beautiful sangria-colored eyes, and I missed his cheeky grin and dimples more than I ever could've imagined. I'd bonded with him the most. I clenched my fists in my lap.

If only I'd gotten to Galina sooner. If only I had *known*.

"What do you say, V?" Ivan's chipper voice cracked through my icy thoughts. "Are you still up for the challenge?"

I tore my gaze away from the empty chair and raised an eyebrow. "I'm always up for a challenge."

Lena scoffed. "You weren't even listening."

"True, but I'm still always up for a challenge." I picked up my knife and fork and dug into the meal.

Unlike most of the food we'd had in Haven, this was a meal fit for a queen. The food would be the only thing I'd miss if I gave it all up. Good thing I had plenty of money to burn at fancy restaurants in Miami.

Ivan grinned. "We may not need it now, but I still want to go after the item you promised to help me find."

Ah, yes. The item he sought in the human world. I'd offered to help him if he fought with us against William, which he did quite well. Even saved me from being captured, only to get taken in my place.

Time to hold up my end of the bargain.

I pointed my knife at him. "You still haven't even told me what it is."

"A one-of-a-kind weapon," he said and quickly shoveled food into his mouth.

Vague answers were my favorite, right up there next to books with tiny, handwritten text. "That sure narrows it down."

He swallowed the entire bite whole. Much like with Mad, I never understood where all the food went. He ate like a starving man, sometimes going back for seconds or thirds, but never gained a pound past slim.

"It can neutralize any type of magic," he explained. "I wanted it for our fight against Galina, but since that problem's been taken care of, now I'm just curious."

Well, that certainly caught my interest. I finished chewing and said, "I've never heard of such a thing."

"Until recently, it's been protected by the *drakony* in Mirdrakona," Pietr said, leaning forward on his elbows. "If the myths can be trusted, anyway."

"Yeah, until some *drochit* stole it, hoping to make a quick fortune." Lena made a sound of disgust.

I pulled my eyebrows together. "If it's a myth, then how do you know it was stolen?"

"A trader from the mountains claimed the dragons were looking for it a few decades ago." She tapped the table with her finger, eagerness brightening her blue eyes even more.

"If it wasn't real, then why were they looking for it? The *drakony* aren't gullible and don't believe in anything they haven't seen for themselves."

"I tracked the trader down, and he said he didn't think it was even in Mirognya anymore," Ivan continued the story. "The human world was the next obvious choice."

Interesting. I wasn't sure we needed a weapon as powerful as this one sounded, but I also didn't want it falling into the wrong hands—if it even existed. Only one way to find out, I supposed, and I happened to be pretty damn good at tracking down missing magical items.

Hurrah for new adventures.

"We'll add it to our to-do list," I said and took another bite. The meat practically melted on my tongue.

Pietr sighed. "Despite the *alleged* claim that the dragons were looking for it, I believe that it was a story made up to keep us out of the dragons' lands. Please don't spend too much time chasing a myth."

I grinned. "Don't want to rule in my place for longer than you have to, huh?"

He gave me a stern look, sending the rainbow colors in his eyes swirling. "Veronica, seriously. It's a bedtime story, a fable."

"As much as the others believe it's real, I agree with Pietr," Liz said, clearly ignoring her sister's glare.

Oleg chuckled but wisely refrained from choosing sides. We all knew it'd be with Liz, anyway, even if he believed in the weapon.

"You'd be better off trying to find the fountain of youth," Pietr added as if he knew I needed the extra persuasion.

He knew me so well.

I opened my eyes wide, trying my best to look innocently curious. "Wait, that exists?"

He leaned back and groaned while the rest of us just laughed.

I would miss seeing this group every day. At least Ivan and Lena would be tagging along for the ride. Morning couldn't come soon enough, even if it meant my heart would break.

Shattered into pieces so fine, I wasn't sure it would ever be whole again.

Thane

I took one more glance around the room that had been my office for the past five years. Most of my files and personal belongings were already boxed up and moved to my new desk upstairs. Not that I kept much to begin with. I wasn't one for sappy mementos.

I reached a hand up to my chest, feeling the falcon charm from Veronica beneath my shirt. Besides the cross my mother had given me as a boy, the charm was the only sentimental thing I kept, and not just because it had saved my life.

Adam met me outside my office just as I closed the door. He wore a ceremonial robe so white it was almost blinding, especially under the fluorescent lights overhead. His smile reached his blue eyes, though sadness tinted both.

"It is time, my friend."

I nodded and followed him down the quiet corridor.

When a reaper ascended in the past, the entire office celebrated all week. Any work that could be put off or delayed would be. Any soul collecting duties would be split, and that was about all we finished.

Ascensions didn't happen more than once every few years, and very few reapers ascended as quickly as I had.

Today, the Saturday morning office vibe was subdued. No parties had been planned for the night before; no meetings were skipped. Everyone knew how I felt about Veronica.

It would be a bittersweet day.

"Good luck, Thane," called a voice from one of the cubicles.

I raised a hand in thanks toward the newer reaper. He and several others stood and watched with solemn faces as I continued down the hall with Adam. The elevator that would take us up to the ceremony loomed at the hall's end.

Before I met that ridiculously stubborn phoenix, I accepted the undercover case to flush out the rogue reaper, Sophia Clark, with the sole intention of gaining my wings. Becoming an angel had been my dream since I'd woken up dead. I hated what my drug addiction had done to my mother, and I felt that I could somehow make it up to her by joining the angelic choir.

That was before everything had changed.

One look was all it took.

I had taken one look at Veronica outside the Star Island mansion, leaning against a railing that overlooked the water. Hair so blonde it was almost white blew back from her face as the salty breeze swept through.

No mask could hide her beauty. No fake contacts could hide the sparkle, the *life* dancing in her eyes.

One look…

And I was a goner.

She made me remember what it was to feel alive again, the way I had lived before my fatal addiction. To smile from actual happiness, to wish and plan for the future, even to regret my selfish, self-indulgent past.

She made me remember what it was to desire.

The elevator dinged, and the door slid open. Adam and I stepped inside, and the door closed.

I never claimed to be a saint, and thankfully it wasn't a requirement to ascend. Because Lord help me, I desired Veronica like no other.

Her mere touch burned my skin, set me ablaze with a fierce need to claim her. I grew hard every time she turned those violet eyes on me. When I spread her legs and tasted her for the first time, I'd had blue balls for days, the likes of which I'd never known before.

She tasted like heaven.

I wanted to bury myself deep inside her warmth and feel her writhe beneath me until she screamed my name.

It wasn't purely physical, though—not by a long shot. Her impulsiveness drove me crazy, but I wanted her to drive me crazy until we were both old and grey, bent over our walkers, and complaining about kids these days.

The elevator door slid open again, and sunlight fell across my face. Raising a hand to block it out, I stepped into the rooftop pavilion where I would gain my wings.

She loved me, and I her. That's all that mattered.

I would give my life for her.

CHAPTER 3

Saturday Morning

After a final farewell breakfast and a quick meeting with Pietr and the royal guards to pass off temporary command, I was finally leaving Mirognya. One month to the day.

The world beneath my feet fell away, disappearing into nothing but the frigid void.

Realm jumping was not for the faint of heart, but it was still better than teleportation via reaper—no stomach-churning nausea aftereffects. My heartbeat thudded once, twice, then solid ground returned beneath me once again.

I opened my eyes and smiled.

Long shadows draped across the building's roof where

we landed, the sun only just beginning its daily journey through the clear blue sky. Miami's unmistakable high-rises towered above us, their windows refracting sunlight in all directions. Honking horns and rumbling engines swept up from the streets below. Nearby, the clunky whir from an air conditioning unit shuddered to a stop.

For the first time in a month, I was *home*.

"Dazhbog's balls," Lena gasped behind me. "What is that smell?"

"Ocean." I inhaled the salt-filled breeze. For all the water that Mirfeniksa had, none of it had smelled quite like this.

"I know what the ocean smells like, you *drochit*," Lena muttered. "The other one that's making my mouth water."

She could only be referring to the Cuban restaurant beneath us. Ivan's realm walking ability had landed us on its roof. I'd considered landing in my safe house, but I didn't know if the penthouse apartment would still be safe. If the necromancer society somehow continued after I jumped ship, then they might have laid a trap for my return.

"Lunch later," I promised. "First, Kit's place."

I'd also asked Ivan to jump us to Brickell City Center under the guise of showing Lena a bit of the human world before meeting my best friend.

In reality, I was nervous.

The last time I saw Kit, she'd tried to kill me. I knew it wasn't really her fault—grief and rage had blinded her. Except when she realized Angela was alive, she had basically forgotten me.

I didn't hold any grudges against my bestie. I forgave her long ago, but I didn't know how she felt about me. Did she think I abandoned her? Did she care that she hurt me, both physically and emotionally?

Deep down, I knew I was overanalyzing the entire situation. The Kit I knew would feel awful for what had happened. The problem was, I didn't know if she was the Kit I knew anymore.

Despite being my best friend, I hadn't known how powerful of a witch she was. As in crazy, terror-inducing powerful. One in a million. She hadn't trusted me enough to share that knowledge, and that stung.

Giving myself a quick shake to let those thoughts go, I led Ivan and Lena to the building's side. Once I was convinced the alley below was human-free, I shifted into falcon form and flitted down. The rustle of their wings followed me to the ground, where we returned to human form.

It was only a mile to Kit's place from here, so we strolled at a comfortable pace while I explained what things were. Things like shops and restaurants weren't a new concept for Lena, but traffic lights, cars, and cell phones were. She hadn't studied foreign cultures nearly as much as Pietr and Pavel had.

We got a few odd looks for our outfits, and one teen complimented our realistic cosplay costumes. I guess we could pass for Robin Hood wannabes with our leather pants and tunics. Large sacks held our weapons and some simple supplies.

I'd have suggested more modern, human-world clothing, but it simply didn't exist in Mirfeniksa. The few things I'd had on me when I first arrived were long gone, and I was way too impatient to have new ones made for this trip. Some of my dresses might have been okay, but Lena would never have worn one.

Ivan had been to the human world, though I didn't know how many times before the day I met him. I also didn't know if he'd ever been outside of Miami. He'd been stalking me for weeks back then, but he could have easily jumped back to Mirfeniksa at any point. He looked around with mild interest.

Lena gawked at everything like a first-time tourist. Technically, she was, but I still found myself smiling at her genuine amazement.

"This is crazy," she said, tilting her head back to eye the skyscrapers brushing a few wispy clouds passing by. "Is your steel that strong?"

I laughed. "It sure is. Though I've been told the witches and warlocks helped keep them from collapsing after some hurricanes."

She shook her head, knocking the beads in her dreadlocks together in a gentle jingle.

The walk to Kit's apartment went way too quickly for my churning thoughts, no matter how many times I tried to push them away. We approached her building's double glass doors on the ground floor.

Flying up to her window and getting her to let us in would have been the easiest option. But I also didn't want to scare the shit out of her and end up getting blasted with her magic. Once was more than enough, thank you very much.

Besides, then Lena and Ivan would feel obligated to defend me. My friends would fight, blood would spill, things would break.

I opted for the safer, less messy approach.

We headed for the elevator. The display panel dinged, and the steel door slid open—out walked Kit and Angela.

Both women were of a slightly shorter than average stature, with Angela a few inches shorter still. And while they shared a similar dark brown hair and eye color, that was where the similarities ended.

My best friend for the past five years almost always wore her hair in a multitude of braids. Today, she wore them up in a ponytail, displaying the shaved side of her head. She often shaved some geeky symbol like a lightning bolt into it. Her Cuban and Dominican ancestry blessed her with a skin color that always reminded me of espresso foam—caramel in hue and buttery in texture.

Only she ruined the blessing by covering herself in tattoos. Clearly, she would be going to whatever hell existed for her kind just for that offense.

On the complete opposite end of the spectrum, Angela could almost pass for a ghost. Her skin was so white it was almost see-through but covered in an adorable smattering of freckles. She had an overabundance of curly hair, which she had pulled into a French twist and secured with a clip today.

Clutching their hands together in a tight grip, both women wore serious expressions that matched their equally serious outfits. While Angela went for a simple black dress and heels, Kit wore a white t-shirt, jeans, and a black blazer with the sleeves rolled up to display the striped pattern beneath.

Someone must have died. My breath hitched in my throat, remembering how close Tony, piano shop owner and a gatekeeper to *El Mercado Sombra*, had come to death. Had something happened to him again?

The two women almost walked right past me until Angela's sad gaze raised to meet mine. Recognition flared to life, and the tiny woman's jaw dropped. She tightened her hold on Kit's arm, forcing the other woman to face me.

I stared at my best friend, hoping with all that I had that she had forgiven me for leaving. Or that she wanted me to come back.

Before I knew what I was doing, I blurted out, "What in Dazhbog's name are you wearing?"

Kit's expressionless gaze took me in from head to toe. Just when I thought my worst thoughts had turned out to be true, she dropped Angela's hand and stalked toward me.

I braced myself for an attack.

Instead, she pulled me in for a fierce hug.

As I squeezed her back, I breathed in the familiar floral scent of my bestie. Her shoulders shook, and it took me a moment to realize she was crying. Sobbing even.

I pulled back to look at her, my eyes wide in disbelief.

Then she slapped me.

Not hard enough to hurt, just enough to surprise me and make a point. "Don't you ever do something that stupid again."

Lena stepped forward, her knife already drawn. She raised it quickly, leveling it at Kit's throat. "Don't you ever strike the tsarina again."

Putting my hand on Lena's arm, I forced her to lower the blade. I gave Kit and Angela a lopsided grin. "We have a lot to catch up on."

"I'll say," Kit said, glancing at Lena and Ivan. She raised

a curious eyebrow at him, then at me. "Let's start with why the hell it took you so long to come back?"

Lena tucked her knife away as a human couple entered the building. We all stepped to the side, out of the elevator's way.

I grimaced. "That's a long story, but it took a while to get Ivan away from William. Good news, that guy's dead."

The couple shot me a disgusted look as they entered the elevator. Understandable for humans, but disgust wouldn't be what they felt if they knew the fae necromancer.

Kit waited until the elevator door shut. "It took you that long to get Ivan?"

"Well, no, but then I had to help bring down the woman who stole the throne from my parents."

Angela pressed a hand to her mouth as she gasped, and Kit's jaw dropped open. It was a look I'd never seen her make before and almost comical.

Now that the flood gates had opened, I kept going, "So then, I had to stick around for a while, until my coronation and getting the realm back in order. Galina, the one I killed, had made a huge mess of things."

Recovering quickly, Kit shook her head. "That still doesn't explain why you didn't come back. You could've snuck away for a few hours to let us know you were okay." She gestured at Ivan. "Surely he would've helped if you asked."

I stared at her. How could I explain my fear to her?

Kit was logic personified. She didn't do irrational, emotion-led anything. Well, besides the whole thinking Angela was dead situation. But she wouldn't understand me putting off the return because I was scared, even if that was only part of the reason.

"In V's defense," Ivan chimed in, "I wasn't exactly available. Pietr had me jumping all over Mirfeniksa, rightfully guessing she would sneak away as soon as she could."

Thank you, Ivan. My knight in leather armor.

She frowned. "Who's Pietr?"

I groaned as Lena snickered behind me. "That's a story for later. First, I need to know how things are here. Are the necromancers still causing problems?"

"No, the Society's as lifeless as it was before William resurrected it," Kit said.

Phew. One problem down. So many more to go.

"And no one is coming after you for your magic?" I asked.

My witchy best friend hesitated and glanced at Angela, who gave a reassuring smile. "No, Adam took care of that problem as only an archangel could."

Relief lifted one of the burdens from my heavy shoulders.

Angela's phone beeped, and she looked down at the message. "We need to go if we don't want to be late." She looked at me. "Is that why you came back today?"

I raised an eyebrow. "Is what why?"

The two women exchanged a nervous glance. Kit reached into her blazer jacket and pulled out an envelope. She handed it to me.

My name was written on the outside, and though I'd never seen him write, I knew it was Thane's handwriting. My hands trembled as I took out the letter.

Veronica,

If you're reading this, then I've failed. Adam gave me a month, but it wasn't long enough to find you. I want you—<u>need</u> you to know that I tried my best, hardly rested unless forced to. We simply have no idea where William's portal led.

By now, I've earned my wings. It'll be better to see you as an angel than not at all, even if my feelings won't be the same. That's why I am writing you this letter. To let you know that you have my heart, that I love you, and I'm sorry I didn't say it before you left.

My lungs tightened, making it hard to take a breath.

I don't blame you for going after him. That stubborn side is a part of you, too, and I love every inch.

I love you, Veronica, for now and always. Never forget that.
Thane

Tears spilled down my cheeks as I pressed the letter to my chest. I was too late.

"Thane's ascension is today," Angela said. "That's where we're headed."

My heart stuttered to a stop, or maybe just time did. Everything slowed to each minuscule moment in which I felt my insides were being pulled out.

"When?" I asked as soon as I could breathe again.

"It's starting right about now, but we can't see him until after it's over, in an hour," Kit said, her expression softer than usual. "No matter what, he'll be happy to see you."

Wait, the ceremony wasn't over yet? Despite his words on paper, there might still be time.

"We have to go." I turned and ran for the lobby doors. Bursting through them, I didn't wait for anyone to catch up before shifting forms and launching myself into the sky.

There was no time to waste. I vaguely heard Kit and Angela yelling from the ground, but nothing would stop me from reaching him before the ceremony was over.

Not even the gods.

CHAPTER 4

Saturday Morning

The Death Enforcement Agency's headquarters was downtown, not far from the Brickell City Center, but I didn't know where the ceremony would occur within the eight-story building. I landed behind the dumpsters on the side of the building to avoid human eyes and shifted back to human form.

At least I had that much common sense.

Ivan and Lena swooped in and shifted.

"Ognebog's flames, Veronica!" Lena yelled, grabbing my arm. "You can't just run from us like that."

My heart thudded with dread. Even the flight over had taken too long. "I'm almost out of time."

Without waiting for another scolding, I shook her grip loose and strode towards the building's main doors. As she hurried after me, Lena muttered something about me being a *drochit* under her breath. Ivan chuckled but wisely didn't join in.

The glass doors slid open as we approached, and I headed straight for the grim reaper receptionist's desk. A cell phone would have been great right about now, but I didn't think I would need one so soon.

The blonde woman looked up from her computer and smiled at us politely. Her brown eyes widened when they landed on me. "It's you."

I didn't know what that meant, but sure. "I need to see agent Thane Munro. Immediately."

She gulped and picked up the phone. "Veronica Neill is here." A pause, her eyes widening even further. "Yes, sir." She put the phone back on the receiver. "You've been invited to join the angels when the ceremony has concluded."

That wasn't good enough. "Where?"

"In the rooftop pavilion."

As I turned toward the elevators, she stood and raised a hand. "Wait, you can't go up yet!"

Nothing would stop me right now. I pushed the up button to call the car.

Flying would be just as easy, probably easier from a speed standpoint, but I didn't quite trust myself to get there without fainting mid-flight. Pinpricks filled my vision, and I took a few deep, calming breaths. It only helped so much.

When the elevator door opened, my guardian angel walked out.

Fiery red hair curled around Jessa's head like a halo, and her smile dazzled. The last time I had seen her, she'd been lying in a pool of her own blood. William's mages had been cutting off one of her wings. Thane and I stopped them in time to save it and her, but her lagoon-colored eyes had never looked so dull as they did that day.

Today, they sparkled once again.

"Veronica," was all she said before I was in her arms getting a giant hug.

"It's so good to see you, Jessa," I said through her curls, "but we'll have to catch up in a bit."

She held on as I tried to pull back. She whispered, "It's too late, love. I'm sorry."

I stiffened. "What do you mean?"

She finally pulled back to look me in the eyes, hers watering. "Once a ceremony has started, we can't stop it."

Her words echoed around my mind like an empty chamber, but I knew Liz had to be right.

Why the fuck would the gods throw a grim reaper and a phoenix together, magically bonding them together, only to tear them apart before anything even got started?

None of my gods was that cruel, and I was fairly certain Thane's had reformed over the last few millennia.

"I don't believe that," I said.

I stepped around her and entered the elevator, Ivan and Lena right on my heels. I pressed the roof button and waited for the doors to close. Just before they slid shut, I met Jessa's teary gaze. Her sad smile just about did me in.

The rich notes of an organ and accompanying choir filled the elevator. Soothing, ethereal church music—meant to be soothing, anyway. I was digging my nails into my palm, trying to keep from screaming my frustration at the endless elevator ride. I definitely should have flown. Lena and Ivan would have caught me if I'd fainted.

The car settled at its destination, and the display dinged once before the door slid open. Sunlight streamed in like a spotlight. Dozens of white-robed angels turned to face us, their wings ruffling with the movement.

Floor-to-ceiling windows surrounded the rectangular pavilion, providing a jaw-dropping view of Miami from above and the ocean stretching toward the horizon. Someone had painted the ceiling to look like the Sistine Chapel.

So unoriginal.

Not even that eye-roll of a thought could steal my attention from what stood at the other end.

Except it wasn't a what—it was a who.

Navy blue slacks and a white button-down dress shirt covered a body I knew was toned to perfection. The sleeves were rolled up to his elbows, showing off his tanned forearms. He'd undone the top buttons, and two gold chains hung from his neck—a cross and my family's talisman.

I itched to run my fingers through his pitch-black hair, cut short on the sides and long on top. Today, a soft golden glow emanated from his entire being, enhancing his already gorgeous features and making his dark blue eyes seem almost lighter. Like a calm sea close to shore rather than the deep ocean whose depth was fathoms below.

Those blue eyes settled on me and widened.

Thane.

I blew out a breath I didn't realize I'd been holding. Gods, he was so beautiful. The mark on my chest pulsed in recognition. Not painfully, but calling to its mate.

The reaper reached a hand up almost absentmindedly to touch his heart, and his gaze flicked to the letter still gripped in my hand.

I smiled.

"What is the meaning of this?" an angel demanded, barging into my view and obscuring the reaper. The male angel was lovely, as most of them were, despite anger hardening his features. Bluish-white feathers fluttered as his wings shifted with agitation. "Who are you?"

I gazed back at him, unperturbed, and let my fiery wings unfold. Gasps rang out through the pavilion. The angel in front of me stumbled back and crossed himself.

Ivan stepped up to my side, holding himself regally. He gestured to me. "This is Veronica Neill, tsarina of Mirfeniksa. Queen of the phoenixes."

A stunned silence fell across the pavilion.

I really did love a dramatic entrance.

Standing beside Thane was Adam Larue, the Archangel and head honcho of Miami's DEA division. He clasped his hands in front of his white robe. "Everyone is dismissed for now. I will call for you once the ceremony begins again."

Most angels followed his command without hesitation, heading for doors leading to the open roof and taking to the skies. More than a few gave me looks I couldn't interpret. Confusion, maybe. Or jealousy, but that was less likely considering their divine status.

Not that I looked hard or cared enough to figure it out, though, because I fixed all my attention on one being, and his on me.

My body didn't know what to do. I wanted to run to

him, to claim him as mine and never let him go. Except I felt glued in place, my boots stuck to the floor. Scared of finally getting to him way too late.

Terrified of the pain to come.

Thane strode toward me, his determined gaze never leaving mine. My bonding mark pulsed harder as he approached until I was in his arms. He wrapped a hand around the back of my head and pulled my lips to his, crushing me against him.

Fire surged within me, flaring out from my core to encompass every part of me, each fiber of my being. The burn was exquisite, and I never wanted it to end. I returned his kiss with passion, folding my wings around us. The smell of cardamom and bergamot curled around me, intoxicating as I breathed him in.

I ran my hands up his shoulders and neck to his hair, gripping those black locks tight. His tongue danced with mine, tasting of salt and heat, of warm ocean breezes. Each touch sent electric pulses down my body and stirred my desire into a feverish pitch. My mark blazed with heat, and a matching warmth from him pressed against the other side of my chest.

Much too soon, he slowed the urgency of the kiss. He pulled back, kissing the sides of my mouth, my nose, my cheeks, my forehead.

I wanted to melt into him completely.

As he continued to hold me close, he looked me in the eyes, stroking my face with his thumbs. "You are too fucking impulsive."

I opened my mouth to defend myself, but he shook his head. His smirk sent tingles shooting down to my already throbbing lady bits.

"I love you, Veronica," he said. "Every impulsive bit of you."

Even before reading his letter, I knew he loved me, had known for some time. I knew because I loved him, too. But hearing him say it, feeling the meaning behind the words, seeing the depth of emotion in his eyes, damn near took my heart out of my chest.

"I love you, too," I said.

Only then did I realize there was no ground beneath our feet. We were only a few feet up, but my wings had apparently gotten caught up in the excitement of the reunion. I settled us back on the rooftop.

"Well, damn girl." Lena fanned herself. "Now I get the urgency. He's hot, and *that* was steamy."

Releasing Thane from my grip was next to impossible, but I peeled myself away long enough to introduce my companions. I was sure I had a goofy smile on my face. "Lena and Ivan, meet Thane Munro."

They shook hands, and Lena gave him a knowing grin as she appraised him from head to toe. Thanks to our girl talks back in Sokol, she knew a little more about him than the others. I hadn't been shy with the details.

"Thank you for bringing her back." Thane smirked in my direction, my body shivering in response. "I needed to see her before…"

Adam stepped into view, his sand-colored hair cropped short like it always was. Like it hadn't even grown out and been cut again because I was fairly certain angels' hair didn't grow or fall out anymore. A white robe covered his lean, muscled figure and matched his wings.

He smiled, though it didn't quite reach his sad blue eyes. "Welcome home, Ms. Neill."

"Listen, I'm sorry I busted in here like this, but you need to see something." I pulled down the neckline of my tunic enough to reveal the dark red bonding mark branding my chest. It practically glowed after that encounter. "My flame chose Thane as my mate. If nothing else, I needed to have this moment before he ascended, even if it means I'm destined to be alone for the next few hundred years."

The archangel's eyes widened.

Thane unbuttoned more of his shirt, revealing a matching, falcon-shaped mark. "What does it mean that I have one, too?"

Honestly, I had no idea. I looked at Ivan and Lena for clarification.

Ivan sighed. "It means it's a shared bond. Both your flames, or soul in Thane's case, have chosen each other."

"Why the sigh then?" I asked, my skin prickling with apprehension.

"Because it's even less likely your flame will move on once he ascends," Ivan said.

My heart sank. It could never be fucking easy for me, of course.

Why the fuck had our gods chosen this fate for us?

Where was a god when you needed to throttle one?

CHAPTER 5

Saturday Morning

Facing the archangel, a flush of anger rose along my neck. I focused on that, needing to feel something other than pure devastation. "Why did you hide all this from me? All of who I am?"

"It is not easy for an angel to break a promise." Adam spread his hands. "It comes with dire consequences."

Seriously? That was such a lame response and not one I was willing to accept. "I'm pretty sure our circumstances were already dire."

Chuckling, Thane slipped his hand into mine. His warmth soothed me, bringing my boil down to a simmer.

Adam inclined his head in acknowledgment. "Maybe so,

but I honored the promise I made to your parents."

"Yet you're talking about it now," I pointed out.

"The promise has been fulfilled. Had you not followed William to Mirognya, I would have told you everything after the clean-up."

Easy for him to say. I had no way of knowing if he actually would've told me. Angels were more than capable of lying, no matter if they tried to convince people otherwise.

The elevator dinged, and the door opened. Kit and Angela stepped out with flushed faces. Angela gave a quick, awkward wave while my best friend crossed her arms and glowered at me. I didn't mean to run away again, but at least this time she could follow.

"No more waiting. Tell me everything," I said to Adam, leaning into Thane's warmth. The reaper's arms wrapped around my shoulders, holding me close. I was home. "What promise did you make?"

Adam's gaze turned toward the windows, and his eyebrows drew together. "We angels have always known about Mirognya, but the trade between realms tapered off over the last century. Your kind prefers a less technology-driven lifestyle than this world does.

"Then, one day, the portals vanished. We had no understanding of why or a way to reopen them until your mother approached me. After learning about Galina's takeover and the attempt on your lives, we decided to wipe the memory of Mirognya from Community minds."

Of course they did. Always thinking they knew best. I wasn't sure if I was talking about the angels, my parents, or both. Clearly, they missed a few people like Jackson Reed, the realm walking hitman Galina bribed to kill my brother and me. He succeeded in taking Maddox's life, but he'd lied to Galina about killing me.

"Why? Why not help my parents take back control?" I asked.

"It is not for us to interfere in otherworldly matters," Adam said, his voice sad as he stared out the windows. "No matter how much we may wish to do otherwise."

I snorted. "And yet you made some kind of promise to my parents."

His blue-eyed gaze turned toward me. "To keep you safe. You are the last of the royal bloodline, and the only thing that can keep the dragons at bay should they awaken and seek war. Your mother did not wish to risk your life or the lives of her people. *Your* people."

"Why would the dragons go straight to war? Are they not morning people?" I asked.

Thane chuckled against my back, muffling the groan coming from Lena or Ivan.

"That is simply their nature," Adam explained.

"They really do love to fight," Ivan added. "The slightest thing can provoke them."

I glared at the phoenix for taking the archangel's side. There were no actual sides here, but my anger didn't go away simply because he had a logical explanation. Besides, the angel did a piss poor job of keeping us safe, and he certainly didn't mention Maddox in that promise.

"So, then what? You let Jackson kill my brother because at least *I* was still alive?" I asked.

Adam's face darkened. "I understand you are upset and still coping with this revelation, but do not insult me by suggesting I did not try to keep him safe, too. I promised your mother to keep you both protected, and I failed. I underestimated Galina's reach."

I knew how he felt. "I'm sorry, truly, but I don't understand why you didn't find it the right time back then? Why keep me in the dark for so long, through all of William's antics?"

"I never expected him to do what he did," he said simply. "I had no reason to believe he could access your world."

That made two of us. It also meant he probably didn't know the things I'd learned since then.

"William knew Galina," I explained. "They planned to take control of both the fae world and the human one after seizing mine."

My phoenix friends already knew this information, but Thane's grip tightened around me, and the archangel stiffened. Kit's muttering included a few, more explicit words than I'd heard from her before, earning a gasp and blush from Angela.

"Blasphemy," Adam said, his tone incredulous. "The Otherworld gods and ours would never allow it."

"I'm not so sure they can stop it directly. Look at what they did to the phoenix world. Galina used magic we'd never seen before, shadow magic mixed with phoenix fire that was next to impossible to combat. And I have no idea what the fuck she is."

Adam grimaced. "She was one of us, a grim reaper."

My jaw just about hit the floor. Two rogue reapers? That couldn't be good for business. And here I thought Sophia was just a lemon. Being a reaper explained the shadow magic Galina had used against me, against everyone, and I had gotten seriously lucky with the bullet. Not much else could kill a reaper so easily.

Was it a random coincidence that I had come across and taken down both rogue reapers? Or were there more to come?

"How did she get away with all of this?" I asked.

The archangel spread his hands in a helpless gesture. "I wish I knew. As hard as it may be to believe, reapers disappear from time to time. Usually, a body will turn up within a few days, but in rare cases, we close the case and move on."

"How did she retain her reaper magic?" Kit asked, stepping closer. "I was under the impression the holy link could be untethered."

"Usually, yes, but we were not able to find her thread. Because reapers' bodies have already died, we link them to us through a new thread of life—the holy link, as Ms. Parker said. Galina's thread simply vanished with no hint of a severance. Knowing what we do now, it appears crossing dimensions to a new realm removes our ability to sever the link. It remains in stasis until the reaper returns."

"That's a huge fucking loophole," Kit muttered.

Talk about an understatement. If word spread, how many other unhappy or impatient reapers would jump ship?

"We were not able to make the connection to Galina until after the portals closed and your mother approached me," Adam continued. "Without Mirilla's help, I could not access Mirognya to retrieve the missing reaper, and your mother was unwilling to do it herself. She would not leave you."

I loved my mother with all my heart, but I was so tired

of all the secrets. So much wasted time and for nothing.

"Why not force Jackson Reed to take you?" I asked, though most of the fight in me had fled.

"A realm walker can jump away from most methods of confinement," Ivan said with a proud grin. "We're not easy to catch, either."

Reaching up, I gripped Thane's arm, still wrapped around me. "How much longer do we have, Adam?"

The angel ran a hand over his face. "Because the process has already begun, weeks, at most. But if Thane does not ascend, he will die a final death."

A final death. Weeks, if we were lucky. The archangel's words swirled around my head, almost meaningless in my grief, which neared all-consuming. My legs wobbled.

Thane turned me to face him and raised his hands to cup my face. His thumbs stroked my cheeks. "Then we'll make the most of it."

As predicted, my heart was going to shatter into a million pieces. This wasn't fair.

"His final death should release your bond and allow you to create a new one," Adam said.

"What if he ascends?" I traced the lines of the reaper's perfectly chiseled face with my gaze. He was like a Roman god come to life.

The angel sighed. "I do not know."

Thane released my face and squeezed my hands. "Death it is."

I shook my head and swallowed the lump forming in my throat. "You've worked so hard for this. You deserve wings more than most, more than Sophia ever could hope for."

He smirked. "She never would've gotten them on her own. That doesn't matter, though. Wings don't mean as much to me as you do, Veronica."

"I'm not letting you die for me."

"There may be another way," Adam said, his tone cautious. "But I warn you, it may not exist anymore, and the chances of finding it are close to non-existent."

"What is it?" I asked, immediately feeling the flutter of hope despite his warning.

"The dragonstone."

I glanced at Thane to see if the word had sparked any recognition. Nope. Just as confused as me. "And that means what?"

"You think it's real?" Kit asked, her expression incredulous.

Lena and Ivan leaned their heads together and whispered.

"I know it is real," the archangel said. "The question is whether it is obtainable anymore."

"Seriously, guys?" My hope was getting the best of me. That or my natural impatience. Either way, I needed answers. "What the hell are we talking about here?"

"The dragonstone is a magical item that grants life to its user," Adam explained. "Created from the tears of a dying dragon king."

Since I had just discovered dragons existed over the last month, I didn't know much about them yet. I wasn't quite ready for that kind of response. "Holy shit. What do you mean it grants life? What exactly does this stone do?"

The archangel met my gaze straight on. "It is rumored to heal all ailments, including death."

My breath caught in my throat. A stone capable of reversing death was exactly what we needed. My hope escalated to heavenly levels before dashing back to the ground in a thousand pieces.

The chances of this thing existing were likely slim to none. Someone would have found it by now if it did. That was what Adam meant by our chances being almost non-existent.

"How do we find out if it still exists?" Thane asked, always the more focused one.

"That will be part of the difficulty," Adam said.

A small, rare smile formed on Kit's lips. "Who better to find it than us, right?"

Leave it to my soul sister to reignite that spark of hope. I smiled. "Might be our toughest job yet."

"Most rewarding, too." She took Angela's hand. "We'll get started."

They returned to the open elevator, speaking quietly as the doors slid closed.

Ivan cleared his throat. "I think I might have a lead. Last I heard of the stone, it was in Mirfeniksa."

Things were happening fast, which was good in the grand scheme of things. Except, I still had a weight pressing on my heart that needed relieving.

The reaper had said he loved me, but there was still so much more I wanted and needed to know about him, about my mate. Whether he would live on as an angel or die, I wanted to know everything that made him *him* before it was too late.

"Wherever it might be can wait a little longer," I said. "I need to talk to Thane first. Alone."

"We'll just be outside," Ivan said, pointing toward the glass doors leading to the roof.

I shook my head. "I'm taking him to my safe house. But no one else. I'm serious when I say alone."

"And I'm serious when I say I'm not letting you go alone." Lena glared at me.

"Technically, she won't be alone." Thane's hand entwined with mine.

The warrior woman grumbled and crossed her arms. "Fine. One hour. That's it. Get it all out of your system before then, or else I'm busting in."

I rolled my eyes. "You mean get it off my chest."

She gave me a knowing look and a wink. "Oh, okay. Sure."

Thane withdrew his teleportation device and activated the black circle that would whisk us away.

Finally, I would be alone with the reaper who had stolen my heart, to tell him everything that I'd been thinking over the last month. To find out all that I could about him and his family, his hopes, and his dreams.

I'd be alone with the man who set every fiber of my body on fire. My body tingled in response.

Oh.

Lena might have been right.

Off my chest...

Or out of my system?

CHAPTER 6

Saturday Morning

As we stepped into the teleportation circle, the void swallowed us whole. Frigid darkness and a total lack of gravity enveloped us. Everything inside me, from my organs to the individual strands of my DNA, pulled apart and rearranged themselves in the brief moment of transport.

Solid ground formed beneath my feet once again.

Based on past experiences, I expected to feel sick, but nothing could beat the warmth of Thane's body wrapped protectively around mine. I reveled in it for as long as I could before stepping back.

My penthouse apartment looked just like I'd left it. The modern apartment's open-concept floor plan and high ceilings made entertaining guests a breeze.

It would be easy to entertain if I ever had any regular guests over, anyway.

Bright marble counters sparkled next to white kitchen cabinets, and a pub-height table provided seating for six. The kitchen and dining room flowed seamlessly into the living room, where my L-shaped couch was as comfy as they came.

Both the kitchen and living room faced two-story floor-to-ceiling windows. The glass panes stretched across one entire wall and overlooked the other Miami high rises and the shining water of the ocean. Watching the waves from my terrace chaise had been a favorite pastime and would be again someday.

First things first.

I took Thane by the hand and led him to the couch. We sat side by side, still twining our fingers together. I drank in the lines of his face, the hard edges and sharp planes of his jaw and cheekbones, the curves of his sculpted nose and dark eyebrows. I never wanted to stop.

Being with him always felt comfortable, relaxing. Like we had known each other far longer than we actually did. After I finally admitted to myself that I had feelings for him, anyway. Despite that sense of comfort, so much had happened in such a short time.

Where did I even begin?

"Turns out I'm a queen," I blurted out.

Because starting in the middle made sense.

He smirked, my body instantly warming in response. "So I gathered. Tell me."

I launched into the story, explaining how the rebels took me in and saw me through the werewolf infection. Every detail of my experiences returned in a flood of memories and emotions, and I shared it all with him.

Well, almost all of it.

I left out a few tiny pieces, like my conflicted feelings for Pietr and the incident in the hot spring. I knew he'd understand, even if it also made him angry or jealous. But there was no sense in ruining this moment over something that never happened.

He knew who Pietr was. Just not *who* Pietr was, to me.

When I finished, Thane whistled low. "Wow. I'd say it's unbelievable, but this is you we're talking about. Chaos follows you."

I laughed. "Yeah, yeah. I'm a mess."

A strand of his midnight hair had fallen across his forehead, so I reached up to brush it back into place.

He caught my hand and kissed my palm, moving to the inside of my wrist. Each touch sent pulses down my arm, shooting through my body in excitement and expectation. His gaze met mine, and the feeling, the raw passion in those dark irises, swept through me like a tidal wave.

I had so much to say, but words would never be enough. I had waited long enough to claim this man as mine. *Mine.*

I pushed him back against the couch and straddled his lap. Drawing feather-like touches across his face with my fingertips, I wanted to memorize every gorgeous feature with my touch as much as my sight.

Slowly, I trailed my fingers down his neck to his collarbone. One by one, I unbuttoned the rest of his shirt, letting my fingers graze his skin as I moved down his stomach. His arousal grew hard beneath me, and his hands gripped my hips, pressing me into him. I did my best not to grind against him in response.

Not yet.

With the last button undone, I pushed aside the fabric and ran my hands up the length of his tanned skin, over the rough edges of his muscles until I reached his bonding mark. I traced it with a finger. His was just like mine, red and fiery—a phoenix in flight. Located right above his left pec, where his heart beat directly beneath.

I met his hungry gaze. His ocean-blue eyes were a storm waiting to unleash, a barely restrained predator circling beneath choppy waters. He knew I needed this moment, and as much as I wanted to memorize him further, we needed each other—completely.

I dipped my head and pressed my lips to his. Sparks ignited inside and all around me, deliciously burning every muscle and every cell of my body. Unable to stop myself, I moaned into his mouth.

He reached a hand behind my back, pulling me even closer. My breasts crushed against his hard chest. I wrapped my arms around his neck, running my fingers through his silky hair and gripping tightly. His cock jumped in his pants, teasing my already wet core.

I wanted to taste every inch of him, as he had tasted me.

I broke off the kiss and moved to his neck, kissing and sucking and licking my way down his collarbone. His grunts and soft moans sent throbs pulsing between my legs. Waiting was going to be so fucking hard, but so fucking worth it.

Continuing the path down his chest with my mouth, I unbuttoned his slacks. I slid off his lap and knelt on the floor in front of him. Meeting his gaze, I gripped the top of his pants and boxers. He wasted no time lifting his hips, and I pulled his clothing toward the floor. His hard length sprang upward.

Not even bothering to remove his pants fully, I leaned forward and took him in my mouth. I wasn't sure who groaned then. His skin was soft and exquisite, and I wanted to please him as much as he did me. More so even.

With my lips still wrapped around him, I stroked his shaft with a hand, lifting my gaze to find his searing into me.

As I flicked the sensitive underside of the tip with my tongue, he leaned his head back and groaned. "You're killing me, Veronica. For real."

Chuckling, I hummed a response with him still in my mouth, knowing the vibration would stoke his already raging fire.

"No more waiting," he growled, his eyes snapping open to zero in on me.

The predator had found his prey.

Still sitting, he pulled me to my feet. His hands moved up my legs and hips before ripping my pants down to my ankles. I stepped out of them as he stood and kicked off his own pants. His eyes roved over my tunic. Before I had a chance to explain the ties on the side, he reached up to the neckline. His biceps bulged as he tore the fabric from my body.

The rush of cool air sent goosebumps flaring across my blazing skin and hardened my nipples.

His head dipped to my chest and captured one between his lips, swirling his tongue around the sensitive bud. As my legs threatened to give out, I wrapped my arms around his head and dug my fingers into his hair. Strong hands gripped my thighs and pulled me up until I could wrap them around his waist.

I reached between us and gripped his rock-hard length, guiding him toward my entrance. He growled into my chest, sucking one last time, before releasing my nipple. As I moved him up and down my slit, getting him slick and ready to enter, he slammed my back against the nearest wall.

His eyes rose to meet mine, the irises lightening to sapphire with his animalistic craving to be inside me. I positioned him at my opening, and he drove into me, hard and deep.

Crying out from the pleasure of finally getting what I'd wanted, I dug my nails into his shoulders. My back rubbed against the wall as he slid out and thrust again. My body stretched to encompass his entire length as he filled me.

His mouth descended on mine, crushing and passion-filled. Our tongues danced together, and I moaned into him with each exquisite thrust of his hips. He pumped in and out, gaining in speed. Heat blazed across my skin.

This was what I'd been waiting for—what I'd *needed* so desperately. He filled me physically and emotionally. My body tingled, on fire with each delicious stroke, and I never wanted it to end.

"You feel so fucking good," he growled against my teeth.

Cold air brushed against my back as he pulled me away from the wall. He carried me to my bedroom and dropped me unceremoniously onto the bed. Above me, his cock was wet and straining for more.

He gripped my hips and flipped me onto my stomach, pulling me toward the edge until my toes touched the ground. With a knee, he spread my legs and slammed inside of me again.

I cried out in ecstasy, and every inch of me pulsated with unrestrained desire. Both of his hands continued to grip my hips, drawing me toward him as if he couldn't get enough.

Clutching the sheets between my hands, I pushed back against him each time he thrust, matching his rhythm. Flames surged inside my core, building into an inferno, demanding to be free.

Everything inside of me tightened and throbbed until I couldn't hold back anymore. I screamed his name as my body climaxed, spasming and pulsing around him. My inner flame shattered outward, consuming me with an intensity I'd never known possible.

His thrusts grew faster and harder until he grunted, pounding into me one final time with his release. "Oh God, V!"

As we collapsed onto the bed, my entire body tingled happily, finally reunited with my mate.

⌇

I stretched, loving the feel of silk sheets beneath my skin. The palace hadn't lacked in its luxury, but there was nothing quite like sleeping in my own bed again.

Somehow, Thane and I had slept through the rest of the afternoon, only waking for more sex. Those times, we were slower and more exploratory as we enjoyed every inch of each other. Then we slept again.

Amazingly, Lena never once interrupted like she claimed she would.

Sunrise was still a while away, but I knew it was early morning based on the slightest lightening of the dark sky outside the windows. I hadn't bothered to close the retractable shades, and the remote was within arm's reach on my bedside table.

Yes, I had finally done it—I had sex with a dead guy. Multiple times, and it was the best sex I'd ever had. I was pretty sure it was the best sex I'd have for the rest of my life, too.

As I turned to slip from the bed, strong arms wrapped around me and pulled me back. Thane's warm body curled around mine, already hard and ready for more.

"You know, some of us still have bodily functions to attend to," I murmured but didn't attempt to leave again.

Warm breath tickled my ear as he chuckled. "Oh, I remember very well. It took several washes to get all the stomach acid out of my shoes."

I dug an elbow into his side until he grunted. "Totally not my fault."

His lips pressed against the sensitive skin along my neck and shoulder, instantly setting my body ablaze. "You glowed a few times."

It was hard to focus. "Hm? What? Glowed?"

"Mmhm. Your skin got so hot, I thought you were going to burst into flames." His lips still on my skin, he trailed his fingertips down my arm, soft and caressing. He followed the curves of my waist, over my hip, and dipped between my legs.

I wanted to roll over and ride him.

"Hold that thought," I said and sprinted to the bathroom.

When I returned, Thane still reclined on his side, head propped up on his hand and sculpted like a very sexy Greek statue. The sheet barely covered his waist.

I dragged my teeth across my bottom lip.

How had I gotten so lucky?

A sword lay where I had been. Except, it wasn't just any sword—it was Lisa.

The blade I'd named after the Russian word for she-fox. Or maybe it was from the phoenix language Yazyk now that I knew the human dialect came from mine. This little blade was sneakier than she looked and had become one of my favorite weapons.

"I thought I lost her." I sat beside him and picked her up, turning the blade to inspect both sides.

"You almost did. I caught a mage trying to sneak off with it. She's been waiting for you here ever since."

I looked up from the blade, my heart in my gaze. "This is the most romantic thing anyone's ever done for me."

He smirked. "So you're saying you're easy to please?"

What a devil. "Not even close."

His fingers trailed up my naked thigh toward my hip. "I beg to differ."

Already, my body thrummed with burning desire. I knew I'd be more than ready if his hand made it between my legs, and those miraculous fingers of his would confirm it.

In one swift move, I had him on his back, my legs straddling his naked hips and my hands holding his beside his head. He was as ready as I was.

"Let's see how well you do when I'm in charge," I dared.

His gaze sharpened, and lightning danced in his stormy eyes. "Challenge accepted."

With a quick tilt of his hips, he slid inside me.

CHAPTER 7

Sunday Morning

The sound of glass tinkling and chairs groaning against wood woke me. I sat up, instantly alert. Thane was already on his feet, padding softly toward the door. For one much-too-brief second, I stopped and admired his shapely backside.

All mine.

I slid off the bed and pulled on my silk robe as I followed him. The fabric didn't cover much, barely falling below my butt cheeks, but it was still better than giving an intruder a full show. Although, that could also be a fabulous distraction.

Laughter drifted down the hall leading to the living room. I recognized those laughs. Sure enough, Ivan and Lena sat draped across my L-shaped couch, soda cans and bags of chips in hand.

"Finally," Lena said with an exasperated huff, eyeing a still naked Thane from head to toe. "I thought I was going to have to bust in there and pull you off each other."

Ivan tossed a pillow at the reaper.

As Thane covered himself with the pillow, his powerful gaze swept over her. "Such a shame you didn't."

"Oh, go put some pants on," I said, trying not to laugh at Lena's dismayed expression. "I was surprised you didn't bust in after your threat."

"I told you I can be nice sometimes." She flipped a few dreadlocks off her shoulder.

Ivan took a sip from his can. "Pavel told me about your orgy fantasy."

My eyes widened. "It was not a fantasy! For a hot second, I thought that's what happened in your 'traditional' bath before a battle."

"Oh, it was hot all right," Lena snickered.

Thane held up a hand. "Hold that thought. I need to know details about her darkest orgy fantasies."

After he turned his muscular bare backside toward us and left the room, I tossed my hands up into the air and threw myself onto a free cushion. "For the record, we are not having an orgy."

"Party pooper," Lena grumbled and grabbed another Doritos bag. "He won't forget that conversation. These things are amazing, by the way."

I shot her a warning glare, but she just smirked and dug into her chips. Based on the amount of empty cookie and chip packages, I would go broke quickly with these two hanging around.

Ivan chuckled around a mouthful of Fritos. "She's right. About the chips and the orgy. Every man fantasizes about joining one at least once in his life."

Thane returned wearing pants but no shirt, giving us all a glorious view of his impossibly defined pecs and a six-pack of abs. He sat on the couch next to me and pulled me onto his lap, holding me around the waist as if I'd flee.

Not likely. I curled my legs up and wrapped an arm around his shoulders.

There was no need for him to ascend—this, right here, was heaven.

I'd fight anyone who said otherwise, including the gods.

"You mentioned hearing about the dragonstone yesterday," I said to Ivan. "What do you know about it?"

"Don't get too excited." He leaned forward and set his empty can down on the coffee table. "I don't trust my source."

I ran my fingers through Thane's dark locks, basking in contentment. "Let's hear it anyway."

"In case the name alone wasn't obvious, the dragons created the stone. It's a collection of their tears, hardened with their fire. Kind of like fireglass. It was a gift for a previous tsarina, one of your ancestors."

Well, that would have been super helpful to have. If only my ancestors hadn't lost the damned thing. "What happened to it?"

He shrugged and leaned back in his seat, crossing an ankle over his other knee and letting out a healthy belch. "No one knows, which is annoying."

To say the least. It was downright infuriating now that I needed its magic to save the man I loved. "I need you guys to go back and look for it."

Lena gave me a skeptical look over the bag of Doritos she was quickly devouring. "And leave you unprotected? I think not."

Thane's chest rumbled against me with his chuckle. "She's far from unprotected."

"No offense, but one grim reaper is not enough to keep this wrecking ball of a phoenix from bashing down walls and stirring up trouble." She waved a red-dust-covered hand in my direction.

Thane's chuckle turned into a full-blown laugh until I elbowed him. Not that she was wrong, but we didn't all need to vocalize our agreement about it. I knew my faults just fine without the reminders.

"Adam will have her guarded day and night," he said. "Check outside."

Raising an eyebrow, Ivan rose and crossed to the terrace doors. He pushed aside the curtains, revealing two angels standing as still as statues and facing the ocean.

He whistled. "I never even heard them land."

I frowned at Thane. "I told Adam to give us some privacy."

"You should know him better than that by now. His idea of privacy does not mean left alone."

I would need to have some words with the archangel. It was nice of him to care and all, but he needed to trust me and respect my wishes. I was kind of his equal now, even if I still planned to find a way to make Pietr take over for good.

"Just because you have extra guards doesn't mean we're going to leave your side," Ivan said as he returned to the couch and grabbed another bag of Fritos.

"Please don't make me command you," I pleaded, almost pitifully. "I need you guys to pursue any leads you can find back in Mirfeniksa. Mama Anya might know something."

I surprised myself with that suggestion. Mama Anya had been the head midwife at my birth, which meant she might be a great lead to start with. And here I thought I was bad at the whole people side of life.

Go me.

Ivan and Lena exchanged a cautious yet optimistic glance.

"I don't know, V…" Lena said.

"I can assure you nothing will happen to Veronica while you're gone," Thane said, wrapping his arms around me even more, his warmth enveloping me. "But you can always return to check on her as often as you need."

Now, that was a smart idea. Ivan's ability to hop back and forth between realms would be super helpful in this search. It would be amazing if I had to keep ruling Mirfeniksa, too. I could come back as often as I wanted.

Although, I had been kind of hoping to be free of babysitters for even a short while.

"I'll go, but Lena stays here," Ivan caved at last.

I glanced between their determined faces and knew that was the best I would get unless I ordered them both to go as their tsarina. Hard pass. "Deal."

Ivan grabbed a few extra bags of chips. "See you soon."

He winked his weird glowing eyes at me, a sign of his impending jump, and winked out of this world's existence.

After a long and steamy—in more ways than one—shower, Thane and I officially got dressed for the day. Back in comfy linen shorts, a tank top, and slip-on sneakers, I felt like a regular Floridian again. I'd have gone for sandals, but I never knew when I'd have to run in my line of work.

It might have been my previous line of work, but old habits were hard to kill. Plus, being a queen came with a target on my back.

I checked Kit's message on my phone and met Lena and Thane in the living room.

On the couch, Lena examined the reaper's cylindrical device (no, that wasn't a kinky nickname for his penis) while he lounged casually, his arms thrown over the back cushions. I smiled at the sight of my newest friend connecting with my mate. My mark pulsed in a contented way.

Mine.

"Kit's still looking, but she's got a lead," I told them. "You guys ready?"

The warrior woman glanced over and did a double-take, eyeing me dubiously from head to toe. "Are those considered clothes in this world?"

I looked down, almost afraid I'd forgotten my tank top or something. Everything was still there. "Amazingly, I'm pretty well covered. Some people wear even less. You'd love the beaches here."

She shook her head and activated the teleportation device, a black circle appearing on the floor. "This thing is so cool. I'd be able to keep up with Ivan if I had one." She turned to Thane. "You think you can get me one of these?"

He chuckled. "Not unless you want to die and start reaping souls."

"It's just not fair," she grumbled, sounding a hell of a lot like me.

I must have been complaining too much. Oops.

He held out his hand and stood. "It can't cross realms like a walker's ability can."

As she handed over the device, her eyes widened with a look of disgust. "Then it's hardly more useful than flying."

"Except this world is ten times larger than Mirognya," I said, joining them at the circle and taking Thane's other hand. "And that's just a guess. It could be even bigger for all I know."

He squeezed my fingers.

I took Lena's hand in my free one.

She raised an eyebrow at me. "You scared?"

I laughed. "No, but unless you want to go flying around in the frozen ether, we have to link to Thane."

Her eyes widened, and her grip tightened. She had no idea what she was about to experience. If I were a nicer person, I'd warn her, but I also felt like experiencing crippling nausea without warning was a rite of passage.

We stepped into the portal. A whirlwind of a moment later, solid ground reappeared beneath my feet.

Only, we didn't land where I expected.

CHAPTER 8

Sunday Morning

I stared at Kit's apartment door—from the outside.

Lena released my hand and bent over, gripping her knees and dry heaving. "Oh, sweet Mokosh," she groaned between heaves, "why didn't you warn me?"

"I'm sorry, but I needed confirmation that I wasn't just being a baby," I said, grinning. I turned to Thane and pointed at the door. "We're outside."

He smirked and tucked the t-port device into his pocket. "An unfortunate incident involving two naked bodies taught me a lesson."

"You're telling me you didn't enjoy the show?" Lena asked, straightening with a wince.

Back to her old self again in no time, as usual.

"Of course I did, but she banned me from teleporting straight inside for a while. Now it's just a precaution." He shrugged. "This works just as well, though not nearly as exciting."

Oh, gods above. I was sure Kit would've stabbed him in the eye had he been anyone else walking in—well, teleporting in that scenario.

My best friend wasn't exactly modest, but I got the sense Angela was more of the pearl-clutching type. Kit would feel the need to protect her lady's honor.

The door opened before we could knock, and Kit's dark brown gaze swept over us. "You going to stand out here all day gossiping?"

I grinned and attacked her with a hug before she could protest. The light floral scent that always accompanied her washed over me, comforting me in a way only she could.

I must have gotten lucky with her only giving me hugs after traumatic events before, because today, she patted me awkwardly on the back and tried to squirm away. Hugs were most definitely not her thing.

"Get in here before I change my mind about helping," she said when she finally extracted herself from my arms.

"You wouldn't dare," I teased. "You love this kind of job as much as I do."

She glared at me as I passed her to enter the apartment. No retort meant I was right.

Once inside, I was swept up into another, though much tighter, squeeze, accompanied by Angela's ear-splitting squeal. How this tiny human had so much strength was beyond me.

I laughed and hugged her back, her mane of curly brown hair tickling my cheek.

When she finally stepped back to look me in the eye, hers brimmed with tears. "I know we don't know each other *that* well, but I feel like I do based on all the stories Kit has told me. You two have had some crazy adventures."

I grimaced. "I'm sure she exaggerated my lesser qualities."

Kit shot Thane a knowing look. "Hardly."

Glaring would only earn me a laugh or an "I told you so," so I pretended I didn't hear her and went for blissful ignorance.

Once we were all inside, I introduced Lena to Angela. Nothing about the two women was similar except maybe their height. Talk about a lesson in contrasts.

Lena wasn't that much taller than Angela, but every move she made, every solid inch of her, spoke to the warrior she'd fought hard to become. Her gaze moved around the room in a constant pattern while the rest of her remained still. A hand rested within range of her closest dagger.

I didn't even think she was consciously aware of her heightened level of observation anymore. She just did it, kind of like breathing.

Angela wasn't defenseless, of course—she was a human witch being trained by one of the most powerful Community witches in existence—but she wasn't a hardened, battle-tested fighter either.

Kit led us toward her computer area. She'd turned a corner of her living room into a workstation, complete with some of the fastest computers this world had ever known.

She'd named them all after various astrological or planetary things, most of which I forgot.

The only one I ever remembered was Hubble because I always thought of bubbly, which always made me smile. Bubbly was far from Kit's personality.

Cute names aside, it was only the best for this technological genius witch—only the best when it came to her gadgets, anyway.

The rest of her one-bedroom apartment was small but cozy, with an open-concept layout. Her bedroom doubled as a gym, thanks to the custom Murphy bed she'd installed. She could easily afford bigger and fancier everything, but being raised in a ridiculous amount of luxury had somehow turned her off of it for life.

To each their own, but if my penthouse was any indication, I sure as hell didn't get it.

Thane and I took the two extra chairs pulled in close to the desk while Lena and Angela sat on the couch behind us. The human witch chewed on her bottom lip and kept glancing at Lena out of the corner of her eye.

"The last known human world location of the dragonstone was in Italy thirty years ago." Kit pulled up a few different windows on the screen. "Originally, it was a gift for one of your ancestors, but I can't figure out if it was in exchange for anything. Maybe your friend will figure that out in his research."

Ivan had been right. Not that I doubted him, but it was good to have confirmation.

"How did it end up in this world?" Thane asked, leaning forward to see the screen better.

"That's another frustrating dead end." She pulled up another window, her gaze tracking through the official-looking text. It looked almost like a police report. "According to Adam's files, it was stolen shortly after your parents left Mirfeniksa."

I blinked at her. "Adam's files? You have access to those?"

Pausing her inspection of the text, she pursed her lips and turned to face me. "Fallout from using my magic again—my *full* magic. Adam talked me into working for him."

Hell must have frozen over. "You work for the DEA now?"

She nodded a bit sheepishly. "Mostly to assist Thane in searching for you."

"You helped look for me?" I asked.

She tilted her head, looking confused. "Of course I did. Not only did I almost kill you, but then I didn't get the chance to make it right. You don't get to run away from me like that next time."

My neck warmed with a flush, an embarrassment I hardly felt. Maybe it was more like shame. I'd spent a month in another world wondering if my best friend was angry with me or even cared that I'd left.

What a dope.

"Hopefully, there won't be a next time," I said.

She shrugged. "You never know."

So true.

"Wait. You two got to run around trying to solve the mystery together?" I asked.

Thane looked away from the monitor to grin at me.

"Jealous? Don't worry. We'll tell you all the stories about our adventures after we track down this stone."

I would hold him to that promise because I was definitely jealous with a severe case of missing out.

"Anyway, Adam's protection keeps the rest of the Community from finding out exactly who I am," Kit explained. "A witch capable of controlling the five elements isn't exactly common."

That was a huge understatement. The last witch able to control all five elements had died over a century ago, or so the rumors said. I had only found out the truth about Kit when she went all blind-ragey thinking Angela had died. Feeling what I did for Thane, I understood her level of grief.

The other Community members present in the fight against William might have figured out what she was capable of, but at least she hadn't displayed mastery of all five elements during the fight. If word of her power leaked, the general Community would fear her, ostracize her, and most likely take out a bounty on her as they had hunted me.

Of course, the coven leaders already knew what she was, but they kept their secrets close.

"Do you believe it's still in this world?" Thane asked, narrowing his eyes as he scanned the windows on the monitors again.

Kit shrugged. "No clue. I couldn't find anything to suggest otherwise. I can track it to Rome and then nothing."

"Okay, so Rome it is." I turned to Thane. "Can your magical rod get us that far?"

His lips rose into that delicious smirk I loved so much. "Baby, my 'magical rod' can take you anywhere you want to go."

Lena snickered behind us.

Rolling my eyes, I tried to ignore the desire squeezing at my core. I wanted his magical rod inside me again. "Yeah, I walked into that one. No need to waste time. Let's go to Rome."

Kit turned off her computer, and the monitors went black. "I'm coming with you."

As much as I wanted my best friend and a super-powerful witch at my side, I was not about to let her return to the one place she hated more than her mother's house.

"No way, lady love. There's no need for that kind of mental torture," I said.

"As much as I agree, my contact won't see you without me. She's extremely private, for a good reason in Italy."

"What's wrong with Italy?" Lena asked.

I'd forgotten she didn't know the whole story.

"The Community there isn't exactly friendly to my kind," Kit surprised me by answering first. Usually, she was tight-lipped about the war. "We were responsible for massacring a fuck ton of humans after World War II ended in 1945."

Lena frowned. "Why?"

"The humans found out about the fae. We were ordered to kill them, even though we'd already wiped their memories clean."

Lena's eyebrows scrunched together even more. "Why kill them then?"

"Exactly." Kit stood. "I'm going. It's about time I faced my demons."

Thane cleared his throat. "I can always provide you with demons to face if that's easier."

I wasn't sure that was entirely true unless he meant a one-way trip to hell. Adam would likely have a fit if we suggested opening a portal like William had done just to let Kit beat them up until she felt better. Maybe they had a whole demon cell block in the Community prison we could use instead.

Kit crossed to the couch and took her fiancée's hands. "I didn't ask you. Are you okay with this?"

Angela stood and leaned forward onto her tiptoes, pressing her forehead to Kit's. Their noses brushed together. The gesture was intimate and sweet on a level I'd never seen my best friend display or accept from someone else. This was true love.

"Yes and no," Angela said. "I'm never okay with you running headfirst into danger, but I understand. I'll be here waiting for you. Be safe, honey."

Ugh, the cuteness was going to kill me if something else didn't do it first.

Lena joined Thane and me beside the desk, and he took out his teleportation device. Kit released her fiancée and came back.

One of the best parts about travel by teleportation was not having to pack a bag other than the ones we brought for weapons. We would be back before ever needing a change of clothes.

I took Lena's hand while Kit took her other one, and I gripped Thane's.

Boom, we were ready for Italy.

Thane activated the circle.

"Bring me back a Starbucks mug!" Angela yelled as we stepped into the portal.

CHAPTER 9

Monday Afternoon

Seven years ago, I went to Rome during a whirlwind of a spring break in college. I loved every second of it, even if I only remembered half the trip or less—we drank so much wine. Although we were on a mission this time, I was excited to see if the city was still as I remembered.

When the ground solidified beneath my feet, I breathed out and opened my eyes. I still had no idea why I bothered to close them, just an instinct against the frigid void, I guess.

There was also the possibility that I was afraid something horrifying existed in the supposed nothingness. I was okay not knowing.

We stood in a narrow alley between two brick buildings.

People walked by without bothering to look at us thanks to Thane's reaper repellent, which he had activated as soon as we appeared.

The repellent wasn't quite invisibility, more like deflection. That ability would have come in handy so many times during my jobs, keeping unwanted human eyes off what I was doing.

"Okay," Kit said as she squinted at her Maps app. "Holly lives in Trastevere. It's about a mile from here."

"I can jump us closer." Thane reactivated the portal.

She shook her head. "I don't want any Community members sensing our magic by using it again. And yes, some of us can sense even yours."

The reaper didn't argue as he tucked away the device. Wise man.

"How do you know her again?" I asked.

She started the step-by-step directions on the app. "We all end up knowing each other over time. She was with me during the war."

"Why such a popular neighborhood if she's trying to lay low then?" I asked.

If I remembered correctly, Trastevere was a super charming, historic area of the city. Tourists made it a point to visit the neighborhood at least once during their stay, thanks to the awesome food and proximity to museums.

"Humans love it, which means the Community typically steers clear," Kit explained, glancing at the end of the alley a few feet away.

With the general hostility aimed at witches here, I couldn't figure out why any of them would want to stay. It was like if a hipster walked into a biker bar and ordered a craft brew. Tempers would flare and fists would fly.

Except that analogy didn't do it justice. It was more like a mouse hiding out in a viper's nest—a fucking death wish.

Kit took a deep breath and led us into the bustling city streets.

Summertime meant the ancient city was packed with tourists no matter the time or temperature. Today, the early afternoon sun beat down on us. A bright sheen of sweat covered most people's faces and soaked their t-shirts' armpits.

As if that weren't enough, street peddlers came out in equally large droves to take advantage of the unsuspecting visitors. The packed sidewalks became an obstacle course as we wove our way through the city.

On every sidewalk, we passed fake designer sunglasses and handbags, spreading across the peddlers' blankets like a gourmet buffet. I liked looking good as much as anyone, but I never felt the need to flaunt it with labels, especially fake ones. In the past few years, I could easily afford the real deals.

Besides, we weren't here on a shopping trip. I continued past the blankets without a second glance.

Lena, on the other hand…

"Wow!" She gasped behind me. "Are those made from real dragons?"

She had stopped a few feet back, gawking at some boots. Based on the gleam shining in the merchant's greedy eyes, she was outside the reaper repellent radius.

I grabbed her arm and tugged her by my side before the man could ensnare her with his hypnotizing words. He might not have had real magic, but the vendors had a way of luring unsuspecting buyers in—hook, line, and sinker.

"Snakes," I corrected. "No dragons here." That I knew of anyway. "They're not even real snakes."

Lena shot a confused glare at the man hawking his wares. "They're allowed to flaunt deception on the streets like this? So openly?"

"Eh, probably not." I shrugged and pushed her onward.

"Then why aren't they stopped?" Frowning, she looked around as she walked. "Where are the city guards?"

I chuckled. "They're called police officers here, and it'd be a full-time job trying to stop them."

Shaking her head, she cast disgusted glances at each new seller even though they didn't notice her anymore.

As we followed behind Kit, her shoulders scrunched with tension, and she cast furtive glances in all directions. She had a right to be nervous.

None of the Community here would be thrilled to see a witch strolling along their streets after the massacre. Thane's reaper repellent should keep most human eyes from noticing us, but not necessarily supernatural ones.

I sped up to reach her side. "You doing okay?"

Her intense gaze continued to shift. "Just being cautious. I don't want to lead anyone to Holly."

"Do you want me to watch from the air and keep an eye out for anyone following?" I asked.

She turned her brown-eyed gaze on me. "Our roles have been reversed."

I grinned. "Oh, good, now you can't complain about being the sidekick."

She rolled her eyes. "I never complained, and I've never been a sidekick."

True on both accounts. She was so much more than that—my true partner in everything but the bedroom.

Hopefully, Thane wouldn't turn out to be the jealous type. Not only with Kit, but I'd have to tell him about Pietr eventually. Perhaps *after* they met.

"Anyway," she continued, "I should be able to detect any Community types if I stay vigilant."

"I'll have Lena circle the air once we get there."

She nodded and resumed her scouring of the streets.

When we stopped at a red traffic light, waiting to cross the street, I drifted back to Thane. His warm hand slipped into mine, sending a wave of happiness through every part of my being. I never wanted to leave his side.

I had turned into a big ball of mush overnight. One good deep dicking and I was a new woman.

Okay, it was way more than once, but still, I was a fool in love.

"They'll banish her if she's caught," he said, bending his head slightly to keep the conversation between us. "Magically. She'd never be able to return unless they lifted the banishment."

"She knows," I said as we stepped off the curb to cross the street. "But she's more worried about drawing unwanted attention to her friend."

"It was a smart idea coming during the day," he added.

Daytime meant less of a chance of vampires noticing us. Unlike other major cities, the DEA's presence wasn't as strong in Rome. Instead, the vampires had taken on more of an authoritative role after the war. They blamed it on the agency's inability to stop the human massacre.

Humans, as in their food source.

Whether that was the actual reason or not, I couldn't agree with Thane more. I'd be perfectly content to go the rest of my life never seeing another vampire again. Ecstatic, even.

A few blocks later, Kit turned down a narrow side street only wide enough for pedestrians and motorcycles. She headed toward a fire escape leading up the side of a six-story building. Standing beneath the ladder, she eyed Thane expectantly.

With a smirk, he reached a hand up to grip the lowest rung. Being tall had its advantages. As he pulled the ladder toward the ground, the groan of the rusted black metal echoed down the narrow street.

I glanced back the way we came, but no one had found the sound out of the ordinary or interesting enough to investigate.

So far, so good.

"She's just three flights up," Kit said and started to climb.

We followed behind her until we reached a closed window on the third-floor landing. She stood outside of it and did… nothing.

Curtains blocked the interior from my prying gaze.

"Aren't you going to knock or hoot or something?" I asked.

She turned a blank expression on me and blinked. "Hoot?"

"Like a special owl code," I said, flapping my hands at my sides like wings. "Don't witches have a thing for owls?"

"I did knock," she said and faced the window again. "With magic."

Of course. My bad.

Lena snickered beside me, and I shot her a death glare. It didn't do a damn thing to stop her grin. I must have gotten rusty.

The curtains inside rustled, and a woman's thin white face with glasses peeked through a crack, just enough to see Kit. The curtain fell back into place, and the window slid open.

"Lena, can you keep an eye on the place from above?" I asked.

"Of course, *moya koroleva*." My warrior bowed and shifted instantly, launching herself into the air.

Finally, a little respect.

Thane and I slipped through the window behind Kit.

The studio apartment was large enough to hold a full-sized bed, a two-seater couch, and a kitchenette. That was it. The ceiling was at least ten feet high, which helped the space feel larger than it was.

A closed door likely led to a bathroom if she was lucky enough to have her own in this neighborhood. Some places provided shared utilities like a hostel. Blues and greens decorated the entire room, from an elaborate rug on the hardwoods to the knickknacks covering the shelf above the peeling cabinetry.

Kit's friend was not what I was expecting. I didn't know what I should have expected, but this woman wasn't it.

Dark brown hair fell straight around her face, almost to the point of being her own curtain. Thick, tortoise-shell glasses slipped down her nose as she eyed us as curiously as I did her. Her skin was lightly tanned, just enough not to be confused with a ghost. Her outfit was some sort of layered monstrosity of mixed dark colors and patterns.

She must have caught my confused look. "I work hard to stay unnoticed here."

With that outfit, I didn't think she would be successful. It practically screamed, *Help, I need a makeover.*

"Why even bother staying in Italy?" I asked.

She shrugged. "This was my home long before the massacre, and it'll remain my home long after. They'll come to their senses someday."

I mean, it had already been seventy years, but that was nothing to a full-blooded witch.

"Thank you for meeting with us," Kit said and gave a quick introduction. "I know it's risky."

Holly tilted her chin down in a show of respect. "Anything for you, *la Strega Definitiva.*"

Kit shook her head. "Not anymore. I'm a basic witch now."

"You gonna drink pumpkin spice lattes now, too?" I asked, unable to resist.

She ignored me. *Rude.* At least I got a chuckle out of Thane.

Holly gave Kit a shrewd look and pushed her glasses farther up her nose. "Whatever you say. I know you're not here to catch up. What can I do for you?"

"The gem known as the dragonstone," Kit said. "From what I can gather, it was last seen here in Italy."

Holly's eyes narrowed. "Why do any of you want the stone of life?"

Kit gestured to Thane, who flashed a charming smile. "He's dying."

Holly's suspicious expression didn't change. "Sorry to hear. I thought your kind ascended once you've performed enough miracles or some such?"

"Usually, yes." His full lips twisted into a smirk. "I've made other plans."

Glancing at each of us, she nodded slowly, sending her glasses back down her nose. "Huh. Well, I wish I could help you, but—"

"You seem to know a lot about the stone," I interrupted. "Do you know where it comes from?"

A hint of annoyance flashed across her face. "Despite the angels' attempt to erase history, yes, I know."

Anyone could claim they knew something they didn't, but the fact that she referenced the angels told me she knew the truth. Perfect. She'd be a lot easier to convince.

"Then let me tell you who I really am." I released my wings, unfurling a wave of fire all around me. She took a stumbling step back with wide eyes. "I'm not just Kit's best friend. I'm a queen. The dragonstone belongs to me, and I'd like it back."

She glared at Kit accusingly before turning back to me. "That would've been nice to know before you arrived. Fine. I can help you. Just turn those things off before you trigger the sprinklers."

After ensuring that I listened to her by extinguishing my wings, she waved us over to some books laid out on her coffee table. They were thick, leatherbound volumes with teeny tiny text.

If she expected me to read any of that, she was sorely mistaken.

"Kit hinted at what you're looking for before you all came, so I did some digging," Holly explained. "I… *found* a daily log in the coven's local archives. Someone was too dumb to recognize the stone for what it was and didn't pursue it."

Phew. No reading required. She had done it for us. Possibly stole the books, too, which meant she was my kind of witch.

"The good news is, you're right," she went on. "Its last known location is in Italy, in a small town called Orvieto. It's not far from Rome, just an hour train ride north." She glanced at Thane. "I guess your mode of transportation is faster than that."

Thane chuckled, then fell into a coughing fit.

I patted him on the shoulder, a smirk pulling at my lips. "Swallow some spit?"

His eyebrows pulled together as he cleared his throat. "Something like that."

"As far as I can tell," Holly continued, drawing my attention back to her. "One of the warlocks involved in the human massacre got his hands on the stone."

Kit's eyebrows raised. "Who?"

"Federico Russo, but that's the bad news. I have no idea if he still has it," she warned. "This could be a dead end."

I slipped my hand into Thane's and gave it a squeeze. "It's a chance we'll have to take."

Holly gave Kit the warlock's address while I leaned out the window and whistled to get Lena's attention. A moment later, a falcon swooped through the open window and landed on the back of the couch.

Holly frowned at the bird as a feather drifted to the rug. "That thing better not shit in my apartment."

Lena tilted her feathered head to the side and shifted into her human form, an amused look on her face.

The witch's jaw went slack. I guess she didn't know everything about the phoenix kind. That, or the angels had been partially successful in their memory erasure. Or maybe it was just cool to see in person.

Lena's narrowed gaze appraised her from head to toe. "You're strangely dressed."

"I could say the same about you." Holly crossed her arms.

Leaning her shoulder against the window frame, Lena grinned and winked.

A blush rose along the witch's neck and cheeks, and she removed her glasses to wipe the lenses. I'd bet it was a nervous habit more than necessity.

Maybe that was how this witch knew Kit. I would have to ask if they'd dated in the past. Good thing Angela wasn't here. Not that I expected her to be the jealous type, but we didn't need any potential drama to complicate matters.

"Off to Orvieto," I said, nudging Thane.

Kit raised a hand in farewell. "Thank you for your help, Holly."

"Uh, yeah, no problem." She nodded slowly and placed her glasses back on her face. With great difficulty, she tore her gaze away from the warrior woman.

I didn't blame her reaction. Lena was a good-looking woman and fierce as fuck.

Thane activated his t-port device and swept us away.

CHAPTER 10

Monday Afternoon

Unlike Rome, the early afternoon hour in Orvieto meant most shops were closed for the siesta. Midday rest was a tradition I could wholeheartedly get behind.

Too bad we didn't have time for that just yet. I added it to my mental to-do list for when I could finally relax and go back to a normal life, whenever that was.

After Lena had recovered from her brief bout of teleportation sickness, Kit pulled up the warlock's address on her phone's GPS and led us through the winding cobblestone streets.

Thane didn't bother with the reaper repellent since the few locals still out and about didn't pay us any mind as we passed. The small town might not have been as crowded as Rome, but I was sure they still saw all kinds of tourists during the popular summer months.

What were a few more?

Orvieto turned out to be one of the cutest towns I'd ever seen. Most of it sat on top of a plateau, kind of like Sokol but much smaller in scale. No giant tree came out of the center, either.

Instead, we passed a very old *duomo* extending toward the sky on one side of town. The massive cathedral's sides were designed with greenish-black and white stripes, an odd pattern that made me think of Beetlejuice's suit. A weird choice but popular in the day, according to Thane.

The front façade was ridiculously disturbing yet still impressive. Detailed sculptures depicted bible stories, ranging from the beginning of creation through the end times. Those pieces drew the most attention. Demons were shown dragging the damned to hell and tortured them in ways that made my skin crawl. The lifelike depiction made me wonder if the original artists had faced real demons.

I had to drag Lena away to keep us moving. She was fascinated by the stories.

The town's roads were mostly uneven cobblestone and super narrow, making dodging the few cars passing through tricky. Most of the vehicles that sped by had scraped up front bumpers, likely from taking turns a bit too tight. Nobody seemed to mind, though, because the drivers sure as shit didn't slow down.

"Does anyone speak Italian?" I hadn't thought to ask earlier, and I didn't know any. I'd tried French once in high school, but that was an epic failure. English was hard enough with dyslexia. "Doesn't your kind speak multiple languages, Thane?"

"Over time, yes," he said. "But I haven't been around that long. Spanish was the first focus in Miami."

"I'm a bit rusty but should be able to manage if we need it," Kit said, glancing from her phone to a street sign. "His place should be at the end of this one." She tucked her phone away as we turned down the street.

The lane ended at a low-walled cliff-side, but she headed for a wooden door I hadn't seen at first. It was tucked between two windows, almost like it was a wall between them. Only the rusty metal door knocker gave it away, and even that blended in.

When Thane deactivated the reaper repellent, Kit raised a hand, ready to knock.

The door swung open.

A short, grey-haired woman with an impressive display of wrinkles hunched over a cane and blinked at us. She rattled something off in thick Italian, flailing her arms and cane in front of my bestie, clearly angry.

Lena's grip on her bag tightened, but she kept her weapons hidden away.

I hid a grin. If this lady posed an actual threat to us, I'd eat my shoe.

Kit bowed her head and said something that must have appeased the woman because her tirade reduced to a grumbling. Kit asked a question and nodded her head toward the inside. The woman shook her head and replied, pointing away from the city.

"*Grazi*," Kit said, though her grim expression didn't give me much hope.

The woman eyed us with suspicion as she closed the narrow door and hobbled down the street, tapping her cane against the stones.

Thane cleared his throat.

I glanced at him, unsure why he was rushing Kit. She was probably just waiting for the old lady to get out of hearing range, though I doubted she could hear us now.

"That was the landlord. Federico died a few years ago," Kit told us. "He's buried in a cemetery at the base of the hill."

"Fuck," I said, my shoulders slumping.

"Yes and no," she said. "Because the city officials had no idea who he was and no one came to retrieve his belongings, they were buried with him."

I blinked. That seemed a little extreme. "*All* of his belongings?"

"Just personal stuff," she said, rightfully guessing my mind went to furniture. "No clue if that includes the stone or not."

Thane cleared his throat again. "Because he was the last known carrier, chances are they buried it with him."

Glancing at the side of the cliff, I grimaced. "Ew. We have to dig his body up?"

Kit nodded. "It's the only way to be sure. But we'll need to wait until dark if we don't want to attract attention."

We leaped to the side as a motorcycle came roaring around the corner. The tires skidded along the cobblestone as the driver narrowly avoided hitting Thane, who hadn't moved an inch. The driver shouted something in Italian and shook a fist before revving his engine and taking off.

Lena smacked the reaper on the arm, but he just grinned down at her.

I kept an eye on the corner for any more death traps barreling through. "You can't magic us up some fake government IDs that grant us permission to dig or something?"

"Even if I could, I wouldn't," Kit said. "I said we *don't* want to draw attention. The last thing we need is any Community members sniffing around what we're doing. Besides, the magical echo would be too obvious."

"We all agree this is probably a fool's errand, right?" I put my hands on my hips. "There's no way a precious gemstone was buried instead of stolen and sold."

"It should look just like a rock," Kit said.

Which meant it was a needle in a haystack if they threw the damn thing out. "You think they buried the man with a rock? What, did they think it was, a precious pet rock?"

Thane's warm hand took mine, sending electrical pulses through my body. "You'd be surprised by what people get buried with."

"If it's a fool's errand, then we'll be fools together," Lena added.

I pressed my lips together and nodded. At least we were all in agreement. "Dig it is."

"What are we going to do until dark?" Lena asked, glancing at the cloudy blue sky.

Kit shared one of her rare smiles. "What everyone does in Italy—eat and drink."

Food in this historic town did not disappoint. We chose an adorable pizza joint called Pizzeria Charlie and splurged on a few bottles of wine as if we were simply on vacation.

When in Rome, right? Or Orvieto.

Whatever.

It was Italy, and the food and wine were amazing. I never wanted to leave.

When we were stuffed close to bursting, we strolled along the streets like any other tourists, waiting for our bellies to settle and for full darkness to hide our nocturnal activities. Clouds covered the moon and most of the sky tonight, drenching everything in even darker shadows than normal.

Perfect for our grave digging plans.

Yuck.

Thankfully, Lena and I didn't need flashlights. Flipping on our ability to detect heat signatures would provide more than enough light to get us through the cemetery.

We stopped to purchase a few shovels and added in some obvious gardening supplies to avoid too much suspicion from the locals. I was fairly certain the wine helped convince the shopkeeper we were just a group of drunk Americans with big plans for our imaginary Airbnb backyard.

Once the majority of townsfolk and tourists had called it a night, we made our way down the winding street that took us to the cliff's base. Crickets played their nightly songs as we passed while our steps were as silent as the grave we were about to disturb. We wouldn't be facing any Risen, at least.

Although, with my luck, it was entirely possible.

Despite our light steps, damp dirt squelched beneath my shoes, courtesy of an early evening storm while we ate and drank. After we slipped through the cemetery gates, I led the way through the tombstones and mausoleums, and Lena brought up our rear.

With my ability to see heat signatures turned on, the headstones maintained a warm, red glow from the earlier sun and guided me through the maze-like layout.

Partway through, Kit gasped and hissed.

My pulse raced as I halted, instantly on high alert for the threat. No additional heat signatures registered. "What's wrong?"

"Not all of us have built-in night vision," she growled. "Try to go farther around the stones or give us a heads up, okay?"

"Can't sense them with your witchy powers?" I grinned in the cover of night. My bestie hated feeling vulnerable, and not seeing in the dark was a huge disadvantage.

She grumbled some colorful phrases an experienced sailor would be shocked to hear and waved me on.

I continued to lead them through the cemetery—this time giving the stones a wider berth—until we reached the newest plots. Because the markings were so faint and nondescript, I almost walked right past the warlock's.

"Here," I whispered. Keeping my voice down wasn't necessary, but it was hard not to. I pointed to the plain grey stone marked with Federico Russo's name. "Do we actually have to dig, or can you just, like, remove the dirt?" I waved a hand to indicate a spell.

"Normally, yes, but dirt is heavy, and you seem to keep forgetting that the magical echo would alert too many Community members to our presence. Dig." Kit stuck the end of her shovel into the dirt, pushed down with her foot, and removed a heap of earth.

Thane and I followed suit with our shovels while Lena slipped into the shadows, keeping an eye out for unwanted visitors. With the three of us digging, it didn't take long to reach the casket, but I still ended up covered in a layer of dirt and sweat.

So much for thinking that we wouldn't need a change of clothes.

The box had two lids, so Kit jumped down and unlatched one half. She pulled out the flashlight she'd bought as a backup in case we got separated and aimed it at the wood.

The hinges creaked as the lid opened, and a cloud of dust trickled through the light. I covered my mouth and nose, not wanting to breathe in skeleton dust. Even if it was just regular old dirt.

Thane chuckled beside me, then fell into a coughing fit. He pressed a fist to his closed mouth, trying to suppress the sound.

Drawing my eyebrows together with concern, I placed a hand on his arm. This wasn't the first time he'd coughed, but I hadn't thought much of it before. I didn't think reapers ever needed to cough, even if they inhaled skeleton dust.

Shows what I knew.

"Nothing on this side," Kit's voice called up. She laid the man's pant leg back down.

I crinkled my nose. Gross. She touched the dead guy. Technically, I touched a dead guy all the time. More than touched. Okay, that line of thinking was just getting weird. Besides, *this* guy wasn't just dead. He was rotting.

Kit closed the lid and reached over to unlatch and open the second. The flashlight illuminated the warlock's face, resting peacefully in death and still pleasantly preserved. Thank the gods for good embalmers. I'd already faced more than my fair share of decaying dead people in my lifetime.

A bag sat beside his head.

Bingo.

My pulse raced and beat loudly in my ears. This was it. We were going to get the dragonstone and save Thane. I hadn't wanted to get my hopes up before, but the moment had arrived.

Kit held the bag up, and I grabbed it while Thane reached down and hauled her out of the grave. Kneeling on the grass, I opened the ties and dumped the contents gently but unceremoniously on the ground.

"Seriously, V?" Kit's tone dripped with disdain.

"What? He's dead. We don't have time to be nice."

That last part wasn't exactly true, of course, but I was way too damn excited to care. Giddiness rushed through me, and I had to work hard to keep my hand from shaking as I rifled through the warlock's few personal belongings.

Except, I didn't find anything like a stone or even a plain rock. Nothing but car keys, an expired credit card, Chapstick (seriously, why bother burying that?), glasses, and a few pictures.

Fuck.

"This can't be right." I went through each item again, placing them back into the bag one by one. My hope plummeted.

When the last item was in the bag, I looked up at Thane. My vision blurred. "It's not here."

He knelt in front of me. "V, it's okay. We'll keep looking."

How he was remaining optimistic was beyond me. His life was on the line, and I had been an idiot to get my hopes up.

I shook my head, the first tear falling. "It's not okay, it's—"

A hiss that sent goosebumps sweeping up my arms stopped me. Not just one hiss, but many. As in a few dozen and, judging by the sounds they made in the shadows, not very old. Still in their bloodlust days and they had us surrounded.

Motherfucking vampires.

CHAPTER 11

Monday Night

Why the vampires were here, presumably about to attack us, was a question for another day. If they were in the cemetery to collect a recruit from its grave, then they should have left us alone, not drawn attention to themselves.

Plus, coming in such numbers was ridiculously overdone. Unless the Italian vampires just liked to do things differently.

I whipped out two knives, and Thane drew his teleportation device that somehow also held his giant reaper scythe, but didn't activate it yet. Reapers couldn't join skirmishes unless directly attacked.

Well, they *could*, but they wouldn't. The agency trained them to follow the rules too well.

Speaking of trained agents, where the hell was Lena, and why hadn't she alerted us?

Kit narrowed her eyes at the darkness surrounding us outside her flashlight's radius and waited.

Brand new vampires weren't known for their patience, so it didn't take long for their creepy, undead appendages to skitter forward and slink closer. The sound was disturbing, like hearing something large and unpleasant moving around inside your bedroom walls in the middle of the night.

A shiver ran up my spine, and I tightened my grip on my knife.

The first one stepped into the light. Pale, shriveled skin covered the length of its exposed body, while black clothes sagged in the weirdest places due to the still-redeveloping muscles beneath its skin. The creature snarled as it looked us over, its elongated fangs gleaming in the limited light. A few more followed.

I guess my days dealing with vampires had *not* ended with Xavier.

One of them hissed something that I thought was unintelligible, but Kit replied in Italian. Thankfully her hearing was better than mine. Or maybe I shouldn't have been thankful because the situation seemed to be going downhill quickly. The snarling intensified, and shit hit the fan.

A flurry of movement in my periphery was all the notice I had before the vampires attacked.

My wings unfurled, immediately catching the closest few on fire. Their agonized shrieks followed as they stumbled away into the dark. I set the rest of my body on fire as well, using it as both a shield and a weapon.

Thane's scythe blazed into view. The curved blade was gorgeous, as long as his arm and lightly glowing from holy light imbued within it. He swept the wickedly sharp edge through necks with ease.

His holy light trick that turned his eyes into floodlights would have been ideal but also would have drawn too much attention from any late-night human eyes.

Come to think of it, my fire was probably a poor choice for this fight.

Too late now.

Kit's expression was grim, but her fists and strength were more than enough against these broods with our help.

Although I wasn't a huge fan of bloodsuckers as a general rule in life, I had nothing against this group besides the fact that they attacked us unprovoked, of course. They were people once, hoping to regain a bit of their humanity—at least in appearances—over time. So I felt kind of bad at how many ended up as ashes and dust.

Such a shame they chose this selfish option.

I raised my arm to throw a knife. Before I let the blade fly, the vampires drew back, closer to the shadows. Narrowing my eyes, I scoured the darkness. I knew better than to trust a vampire.

Something was coming.

A scuffling in the dirt and grass came from the left, and an older vampire with sharp, chiseled features strode into the light. Dark eyes scowled beneath jet-black eyebrows and hair. Add in the leather jacket and extra tight jeans that provided a clear indication of his well-endowed... *features,* and he was a dream come to life.

More like a nightmare.

Considering how handsome he was, he might have been a Master or close to it.

In the nightmare vamp's fist, he clenched Lena's dreadlocked hair, practically dragging her along behind him as she tried to keep her balance in the mud. Chains bound her arms behind her, and a gag covered her mouth. A large red welt rose from her temple, and her bright blue eyes were wild with anger.

The vampire tossed her to the ground at his feet.

She fell hard on her knees before turning her glare up at him. Putting a boot on the ground, she made to rise again.

His foot moved in a blur as he kicked her back to the wet dirt. She might have been a trained warrior and a strong phoenix, but she'd never faced vampires before. An older one like this guy would be tough for anyone to take down, even without being bound.

"Hey, Bloodsucker. Does picking on a tied-up woman make you feel like an even bigger dead guy?" I taunted, raising my knives.

"You will come with us, or you will all die," Nightmare replied in a thick Italian accent.

Thane's eyes glowed with a soft white light. Oh, look, his holy light had a dimming switch. Good to know.

"You are making a serious error in judgment," he warned, his tone harsh.

The vampire hardly glanced at the reaper even though his skin steamed beneath the holy gaze. He kept his attention on me and my fiery wings. "We do not tolerate trespassers in our gardens. You will meet with the king and queen, or you will die."

Did the European Vampire Association think they were growing vegetables or something? Maybe fruits would be a more accurate description since they were seedy little fuckers.

Did they make their own special mix of Bloody Mary's, too?

Gross. No one in their right mind would ever make an analogy between a cemetery and a garden or between a corpse rising from a grave and seeds sprouting into flowers.

That was one more reason why I would never trust a vampire—they were fucking nutjobs.

"We didn't know we were trespassing. Let my friend go, and we'll leave." I lowered my knives. He wasn't worth the fight.

Nightmare's brooding gaze bored into mine, and a feather-light tickle fluttered in the back of my mind. He was trying to *influence* me with his near-hypnotic vampire ability. "You will meet with the king and queen, or you will die. It is not up for debate."

This guy was really into repeating himself. I burned his influence out, enjoying the quick flash of a wince crossing his face. He wasn't nearly as strong as Xavier had been.

"I don't do well with threats," I said.

The vampire bent to grab Lena's arm and hauled her back to her feet. Before I could even take a breath, he had her neck bent to the side, displaying his fangs in a vicious snarl at her neck. Beneath his lips, her artery pulsed with life.

"How is this for a threat?" he asked, grazing her skin with his bottom lip.

I glared at him and took a step forward only to find Kit's hand on my arm, pulling me back.

"Veronica, let's be civil since they've clearly forgotten how to treat foreign Community guests," she said, narrowing her dark eyes at the vamp.

Smiling, he let go of Lena, who stumbled forward from the unexpected release. A flash of red passed through his irises. Younger vampires skittered into the light, dragging chains behind them.

"Oh, hell no," I said, raising my knives again.

"Is this really how you welcome guests?" Kit accused Nightmare.

"You are not guests," he said. "You are trespassers who are lucky to be still alive."

Thane retracted his blade into the t-port device. His holy gaze continued to draw steam from the vampire's skin until he flicked the ability off. "Chain us if you must, but rest assured, the agency will hear of this egregious behavior."

Nightmare finally looked at the reaper and grinned. "I will be sure to shake in my boots."

We allowed him to bind our wrists and ankles like prisoners and followed them through the gravestones. I pushed some heat into the links, testing them, but a magical prevention potion must have coated the metal.

Besides the metal clanking together, it was eerily quiet, as if all the nocturnal animals and insects had hidden away with the vampires' arrival.

Outside the cemetery, the vampires loaded us into the back of a windowless van—like that wasn't totally ominous. A few climbed in with us while the rest melted away into the shadows.

Despite the lack of side windows in the van, only a metal grate separated the back from the front seats, allowing us visibility out the windshield.

As we sped through the countryside, none of us spoke. Lena's grumbling behind the gag died out after the first ten minutes, and she spent the remaining time glaring at the back of the driver's head.

Nightmare, the vamp driving, hardly braked once, not even for stop signs. He killed the van's headlights miles away from wherever we were headed.

Dim, cloud-covered moonlight guided the van as we wound our way up a long driveway, spiraling around a large hill. At the top, the Italian villa serving as the European Vampire Association's primary nest sprawled across a rolling hillside. No lights came on outside the building as we parked.

Things were looking more and more promising with each second. If by promising, I meant extremely dangerous and downright deadly.

The back of the van opened, allowing a fresh breeze to blow in and clear the vampires' stench from my nose. I had forgotten how bad the newer ones smelled, and I prayed to sweet mother Mokosh that this would be the last time I'd ever be in such proximity again.

Still chained together, I followed Thane and Kit out of the van and flipped on my ability to see heat signatures. The warmth from the ground seeped into view, coloring the mansion in red, green, and blue. Tiles covered the roof, and ivy crept up the walls. Judging by the simplistic design and doors, I guessed we had pulled up to the back of the building.

The villa would have been beautiful during the day,

when the sun kept vampires from crawling over it as they did now. The number of bloodsuckers I counted as they skittered around in the dark sent a shudder rolling across my shoulders.

This was the stuff from which horror films were created.

A nudge at my back got me moving toward the open door. Once we entered the darkened villa, the handful of vampires with us unshackled our hands and feet. They probably figured we were grossly outnumbered within their walls and wouldn't try anything crazy. Sadly, they were right.

For now.

At last, they ungagged Lena.

She dropped to a muddy knee in front of me and bowed her head. "Tsarina, I failed you."

I snorted. "Oh, stop. Vampires are like cockroaches—they're hard to kill and love dark, dank places like sewers. Now you know better for next time."

Thane barely hid his laugh behind a cough.

Although they might not understand English, the newer vampires hissed as they must have guessed my tone's meaning. Their fangs were hardly visible in the limited light, rendering them far less scary than they thought they were.

"I hope, very much, that there will be a next time." She stood and scowled at the vampires, wisely keeping any other thoughts to herself.

Only one of us needed to knock on Death's door tonight, and that would be me.

Nightmare led us down a hallway, where our shoes tapped loudly against the marble floor. The lights were still off, but heat rose from the paintings lining the walls.

Someone must have turned off the uplighting just before we arrived.

Sneaky bastards—I was sure they just loved making non-vampiric visitors feel vulnerable.

Beside me, Thane seethed. Anger drifted off him like a furnace about to combust. Not only had we been unjustly attacked, but then we had to wait over an hour in a bumpy, uncomfortable, super smelly van just to get to the mansion. All while chained up like animals. He had stewed the entire ride.

Not that I blamed him. I was mad, too, but the vampires had provided a perfectly timed distraction from the failed grave robbery and still missing dragonstone.

Slipping my hand into his, I leaned closer to whisper, "Do you think it would help to let them know who I am?"

He shook his head.

Vampires had extremely good hearing despite their being dead status. Asking my question had been enough of a risk. Judging by the slightest tilt of Nightmare's head in front of us, he knew we were whispering.

Now, I had seen some luxurious Miami digs in my day, but he led us into a room that took my breath away. And that was before I noticed the two ancient vampires sitting on thrones watching us.

Red velvet wall panels embroidered with black roses and wickedly sharp thorns covered the room's length, and parquet floor tiles displayed a lovely chevron pattern. Encased in large, gilded frames, several hand-painted portraits lined the walls—previous rulers judging by their crowns and fangs.

Multiple sparkling chandeliers hung from the vaulted

ceiling while an ornate gilded canopy arched over the thrones, providing the room with a very theatrical feel. Both chairs featured high, arched backs and upholstered armrests covered in crimson silk damask.

For the first time since dealing with vampires on a first-name basis, I caught an inkling of just how far back in history these bloodsuckers went. This was a godsdamn medieval throne room that would rival the Queen of England's. It was entirely possible that vampires influenced wars and were the real cause behind the dark ages.

I didn't know anything about the dark ages, but it was a fun thought.

The king and queen's expressions were icy and still as we approached. Judging by their nearly glowing white skin and overall radiant beauty, these two had become vampires several millennia ago. They were almost difficult to look at directly.

The king's dark brown gaze stared intently at our party as if he was able to see down into our souls. He couldn't actually do that, but a shiver rolled up my spine all the same. A neatly trimmed dark goatee hugged his chin and lips handsomely, but his nose seemed almost too large for his face.

Except instead of lessening his striking look, it somehow made him more attractive. Approachable, even if his eyes warned otherwise.

A gold crown studded with precious gems sat atop wavy chestnut hair that fell to his shoulders. Chunky rings made of equally rare gems covered his large hands, which rested on the arms of his throne.

His black suit fit his trim figure like it was an extension

of his body even while sitting. He wore it so naturally, so effortlessly; he must have been born in that suit. A blood-red silk tie stitched with tiny black roses matched the rest of the room's decor, and shiny black Testoni Oxfords hugged his feet.

I only knew the brand because Joe, my favorite coffee shop customer, wore the same as an homage to his home country.

Beside him, the queen also bedazzled in a gold crown and jewels, including a rose-shaped ruby necklace that drew the eye to her sharp collarbones. Her blonde hair was lighter than the fae queen's rich golden locks but equally as drool-worthy in its luscious waves. Light brown eyes regarded us beneath arched eyebrows. No frown lines appeared on her doll-like face, but I got the distinct sense she was less thrilled than the king at our arrival.

She also dressed far chicer and more modern than I'd expected. A black silk dress with thin straps and a cowl neck collected low between the swell of her breasts and draped over her body, enhancing the dangerous curves beneath.

The bottom hem of the dress fell to her knee, displaying strappy black stilettos reaching just past her crossed ankles. A set of gold chains embellished with ornamental jewels, crystals, and beadwork decorated the sandals' front.

"Their Royal Majesties, King Vincenzo Morelli, and Queen Bianca D'Angelo," Nightmare announced, bowing before them.

He then introduced us as foreign intruders. I couldn't roll my eyes hard enough.

The queen's high-pitched voice lashed out first, "An American grim reaper and two *extinct* phoenixes. What a rare treat." Her lip curled as she glanced at Kit. "And a witch." Her last word dripped with disdain.

She didn't need proper introductions to know what Thane and Kit were—she could sniff that truth out. But there was no way she'd know a phoenix by scent, which meant she knew who we were before we arrived.

"This isn't a pleasurable visit," Thane said, his voice tight with anger. He gave our names and relationships with the agency, leaving out Kit's full name. "We were attacked unprovoked by some of your newest creations."

"Were you now?" Bianca asked.

"Don't insult us by insinuating you aren't aware." Thane narrowed his eyes. "You can smell their deaths all around us."

Being able to smell death was a gross thought. Who knew—death might be a nice scent to vampkind, like an expensive perfume, which was an even grosser thought.

"True, but to say the attack was unprovoked is not accurate," she said. "You were digging in one of our gardens without permission."

There was that horrible analogy again. Vampires weren't fucking vegetables, even if they did get planted like a seed… in the dirt…

"Your people didn't wait for an explanation or identification before they attacked," Thane said. He gestured toward Lena, who still sported a giant bump on her forehead and a vicious glare. "They ambushed an associate of the DEA."

The queen tilted her head to the side. "And how do you plan to prove that?"

"You would question a reaper's word?"

"You would question a queen's?"

Thane chuckled, though it was a dark sound. "When she's wrong, yes."

The few other bloodsuckers in the room hissed at the insult, but the king waved it away.

"Gabriel, is this true?" Vincenzo asked the older vampire who had given us the ultimatum in the cemetery.

I thought the name Nightmare suited him far better than the angelic one.

Gabriel's nostrils flared. "The younglings made a poor choice before I arrived."

"And what of the ambush?" Vincenzo demanded.

"The phoenix is heavily armed," the other vampire said, his eyes hard and unyielding under his king's gaze. "I decided to protect our own first."

Vincenzo heaved a sigh. "It appears the reaper is correct. Please accept our most sincere apologies. We will ensure this does not happen again."

Thane nodded. "We appreciate your understanding—"

"However," the king interrupted, his dark gaze fixated on Kit. "We have something else to discuss now."

She held her head high. "You know who I am."

The hairs on the back of my neck raised. Something was happening. I didn't know what, and that scared the fuck out of me.

"We thought we made it clear what would happen if you stepped foot in Italy again." His voice and demeanor were calm despite the threat laced around each word.

"Some things are worth risking your life for," Kit said.

Wait, what?

"Hold up. What are you talking about?" I asked.

Bianca's red-lipped smile was sinister. She clearly hated witches more than her companion. "Your witch friend is known here as *la macellaia*. The butcher. Unlike others of her kind, the butcher's presence in Italia comes with a death warrant."

CHAPTER 12

Monday Night

Before my brain had a chance to catch up with what the vampire queen had just said, two gangly vampires stepped forward from the shadows. Drool dribbled down one's chin as they approached Kit with chains. Worse, she didn't even try to struggle.

This was not happening.

I raised my hands. "Listen, this is either a massive misunderstanding or something we can work out."

"There is no misunderstanding with *la macellaia*," the queen sneered, a hint of elongated fangs protruding from her top lip. Considering her age, the fang slip was surprising. "She knew her fate as soon as she stepped foot on our soil."

Kit's sad brown gaze met mine as they shackled her wrists again. "It's okay, V. Like she said, I knew the risk. I need to face the consequences of my actions."

Lena sucked in a sharp breath behind me, and Thane slipped his hand into mine, holding me tight.

"By dying?" I asked, my throat constricting with the idea of losing my friend. "You've suffered enough for several decades now. That's worse than death."

The two vampires tugged on the chains binding her and led her away.

"We'll figure this out, Kit!" I yelled as she disappeared out the door.

Fucking fuck. I *hated* vampires. Always fucking up my life.

But godsdamn Kit should have told me they'd execute her if she stepped foot in Italy. That was a huge fucking gamechanger. There was no way I would have let her come knowing that teeny tiny little detail. I couldn't lose my mate *and* my best friend.

I whirled to glare at the vampire leaders. "What will it take to free her?"

Vincenzo's dark gaze swept over me, lingering on my dirt-stained legs and arms. Had I known I'd be facing royalty today, I would have gone for a little more coverage than shorts and a tank top. The dirt was probably a turn-on for his kind, with the whole clawing-themselves-from-their-own-graves thing.

Or, you know, *gardening.*

"There is nothing you can offer that would persuade us to change our minds."

Ah, but they didn't know who I was yet. Not the whole

truth, anyway.

I smiled, though it was far from a friendly expression. "We haven't been properly introduced. I'm Veronica Mirilla Neill, daughter of Mirilla Vasiliev, tsarina of Mirfeniksa. Queen of the phoenixes."

Bianca and Vincenzo's matching dubious expressions weren't a complete surprise, so I showed them my wings. Heat blazed against my back.

Their eyes widened, the only sign that the effect fazed them. No other creature in our worlds could sprout wings of fire at will. Just me, and they had really come in handy.

"I must have *something* you want," I said.

The queen leaned toward her mate. Her lips didn't move, but I knew she whispered something to him so low I couldn't hear. In times like this, I was sure they wished their telepathic ability extended beyond their own creations.

Vincenzo's eyes turned thoughtful. "There is something we will accept. It is called *scatola del cuore*, a heart box."

Another fucking vampire wanting another fucking box.

I glanced at Thane, who looked as bewildered as I felt. "I have no idea what that is."

"And you don't need to know," Bianca said.

Letting go of my hand, Thane fell into a fit of coughing, his fist held at his mouth.

"I don't have time to play games with you," I said, my chest tightening with each racking cough.

"Oh, this is no game," she said, leaning forward, hunger gleaming in her eyes. "We know where it is."

Exasperated, I waved my hand. "Out with it."

A low hiss behind me raised the hairs on the back of my neck. Her guards must not like how I'd spoken to her. Too bad for them because I wasn't going to show her respect if it wasn't reciprocated. I was her equal.

Besides, they were lucky it was with words and not blades.

"Octavia Parker has it," she finally answered.

I blinked at her. Octavia Parker, as in Kit's mother? It couldn't possibly be that easy, or else the vampires would have worked out a deal by now. "Seriously?"

"Seriously," she mimicked me, though I was pretty sure she added more sass than I'd given.

"If you haven't been able to buy it from her, what makes you think we can?" I asked, regally choosing to ignore her insulting tone.

"You can give her back her daughter's life. What could be more priceless than that?"

Never trust a vampire. That was one lesson my parents taught me that I would always remember. Something told me there was more to this item than I thought, and I wasn't sure this would end well. I also wasn't so sure Kit's mother would care enough to bargain with a vampire.

But, like Thane, my best friend was more precious than anything to me. I would have to hope she exaggerated her stories about her mom. We'd figure out whatever came next together.

We had to.

"I want to see Kit before we go," I said.

"Of course." The king's pupils flashed red, and another newer vampire slunk out of the shadows. "Rest assured. Despite the atrocities she committed against the sacred humankind, we will not harm your friend. Unless you fail in retrieving the box, of course."

With great difficulty, I withheld my eye roll and forced a smile. Sacred humankind, my ass—they meant lunch.

I reached for Thane's hand again.

"The reaper must stay here while you visit the witch," Vincenzo added.

"Why?" I frowned, not liking that idea one bit. For all I knew, they could be planning to take us down once separated.

"One of you may get the unwise idea to teleport *la macellaia* out of Italy."

Fucking vampires. That thought had crossed my mind.

I feigned offense and clutched my nonexistent pearls. "We wouldn't dream of offending the EVA that way. Very well, my guard will accompany me."

I squeezed Thane's hand before letting him go. Glowering at every vampire she could, Lena moved to my side, and we followed our gangly guide out of the room.

A few twists and turns later, the vampire stopped its scrambling gait at a heavy steel door that groaned when it opened. The bloodsucker ushered me through but thankfully didn't follow me inside. Although, if this *were* a trap, I wouldn't be nearly as thankful when I burned the whole place to the ground.

Darkness engulfed most of the small room despite the flickering lantern on the wall next to the door. A turned-over bucket covered in dirt and mold—let's just pretend that's all it was—sat in one corner, and a pile of brittle, brown hay took up the back wall.

A dark and dingy dungeon wasn't exactly unexpected, but it still gave me the heebie-jeebies knowing my best friend would be staying down here for even a short time. She sat on the floor with her knees pulled to her chest and her arms wrapped around her shins.

While I would have preferred that they gave her a cot to sit on, I didn't think one would even fit in this cell. At least they didn't chain her to the wall as they clearly had with previous tenants.

The walls and floor weren't brick or stone as I expected. They were steel like the door. I touched the closest wall and tried to heat it. Nothing. It was a completely magic-resistant room.

Turning to Lena, I held up my hand. "Wait outside, please."

If this turned out to be a trap, then *she* could burn this whole place to the ground.

Kit's gaze flicked to me as I approached, but she didn't raise her chin from her knees. "Don't you dare do anything stupid. Lena, you make sure of it."

Lena chuckled outside the door. "I'm well prepared to handle her antics."

"You know me too well." I tried to smile, but it was shaky. "If you don't want me doing it, then I need you to bust yourself out."

Kit shook her head. "I can't."

"Yes, you can. You're crazy powerful." So powerful, she could have easily killed me before I went stumbling through that portal.

"That was before Angela helped me bind my magic."

My jaw went slack, and I almost had to lean against the wall for support. "How do we undo that?"

What I really wanted to ask was why she had done something so dumb.

Her smile was sad. "We don't. For one, we'd need Angela, and two, she'd never forgive me."

"I think she'd understand if she knew the other option was your death," I pointed out. "Besides, if we don't get Angela, then I have to go see your mom."

Her head snapped up, and she narrowed her eyes. "What? Why?"

"She's got something the vampires want."

Kit laughed. She actually fucking laughed. "Oh, she's going to love that. Good luck. She won't want to lose that leverage. You'll have to pry it out of her cold, stiff hands."

I wrinkled my nose. "Gross. You don't think she'll give it up to save your life?"

Her smile turned grim. "No. Not without something in it for her, and my life doesn't count. Any request will have dire consequences. Remember that."

Through the doorway, Lena and I exchanged an apprehensive glance. I wasn't sure what could be more dire than Kit and Thane's imminent deaths, but yeah, okay. I'd try to keep it in mind.

If it came down to Octavia's life or Kit's, though, her mom would be toast.

After I exited the cell, the door clanged shut. My last image of her was as we found her—chin resting on her knees, her gaze sad and distant. Alone. It threatened to break my already fragile heart.

Returning to the foyer outside the throne room with misty eyes, I found Thane waiting, a cup in his hand. I raised an eyebrow in his direction.

He raised the cup in a half-hearted toast before draining the contents.

Both of my eyebrows shot to my hairline. I'd never seen him eat or drink anything before. My mouth went dry, though not from thirst.

A reaper needing something to drink was a clear sign of a dying reaper. My heart sank into a pit of despair as I suddenly understood his coughing fits.

His body was starting to give out on him.

Fuck.

How much longer did we have?

The air turned stifling. Moisture collected on my forehead and chest, and pinpricks darted across my vision. Adam said we had a month, but at this rate, it might not be that long. Or if he did last a month, how long until he wasn't walking on his own anymore?

How long until his lungs gave out?

I had lost a month with him already while I was in Mirognya. I didn't want to lose another by chasing down some magical relic that might or might not exist anymore. That might not do what we hoped it would.

Were we wasting what precious little time we had left?

CHAPTER 13

Monday Night

Thane held out his hand, stirring me from my dark thoughts. He'd already activated the teleporting circle. "Ready?"

To take his hand and be by his side?

Always.

I clasped his hand, allowing the warmth of his touch to take the edge off my worst worries. The black spots in my vision faded. He was here with me now, and I had to fight, to keep going so he could be with me for always.

Lena took my other hand, and the world fell away.

A moment later, soft earth formed beneath my feet. Crickets and cicadas sang in harmony, hidden among the tall, leafy green trees surrounding us. I took a deep breath and opened my eyes. The setting sun stretched toward the western horizon.

We'd left Italy in full dark, sunrise only a few hours away, and jumped back in time to watch the sunset the day before in Virginia.

Time zones were so weird.

Lena gagged and spat next to me. "That is such a rough way to travel."

I smiled. "Your body will get used to it."

"How long does that take?" she grumbled.

Thane bent over, hands on his knees, and heaved. Red splatters marked the green grass beneath him.

The breath caught in my throat. Blood? Already? This was progressing way too fast.

Standing straight, he rubbed the back of his hand over his mouth and grimaced at the red streaks left behind.

Lena dug into her bag and withdrew a flask before handing it to him. He took a drink, swished, and spat, then poured a little over his hand. It washed the evidence away.

"Adam warned me that teleporting is not kind to the decaying body," he said, handing the flask back.

"He did? Why didn't you tell me?" As dread filled my stomach, the delicious Italian food from earlier churned and threatened to rise. "Lena and I have wings. We could've flown."

A smirk pulled at his cheek. "To Italy?"

I swallowed down the lump in my throat. "We could've picked up a new set of teleporting wheels."

"And make me miss all the fun?" The lines of his jaw moved as he clenched his teeth. He nodded toward the trees.

"I'm good. Let's go."

Ready to argue with him or call him a cab, I made the mistake of glancing in the direction he pointed. My jaw dropped open. Even Lena whistled.

I knew Kit came from a wealthy family, but damn.

A few steps through the trees deposited us at the base of a slightly sloping, grassy hill. At least an acre's worth, if I had to guess. Stone steps dug into the hillside, providing an easy way up and down, especially when the grass glistened with moisture like tonight. Either we'd missed a storm, or the sprinklers had done their job well.

For now, I'd drop the argument with Thane. He'd already done the damage by teleporting here. But after we got this heart box or died trying—because that was the only way I was leaving empty-handed—I would convince him to return to Miami and stay there.

We started our ascent, gazes glued to the hill's top, where a two-story white house sat. A mansion, really. Four Greek revival-style columns held up the central front portico, flanked by two roaring griffin statues. Judging by how lifelike those creatures appeared the closer we got, someone in Kit's ancestry, or maybe the architect, had been to Mirognya.

The mansion's two wings stretched right and left from the portico, ending at double galleries with ornate black metal brackets and balustrades that reminded me of New Orleans. Ivy crept up the house sides to wrap around the railings' ironwork.

Horses neighed somewhere off in the distance, and within a nearby workshop constructed in the same style as the main house, metal striking metal indicated a blacksmith was hard at work.

Talk about an upbringing.

I hadn't realized how sheltered I'd been growing up. Living for centuries, or longer, really gave some members of the Community a leg up in life. Octavia Parker's house was proof of that.

Remembering my parents' smiling faces on Christmas mornings, I wondered which life they had preferred.

As we approached the relatively simple double front doors—simple in comparison to the rest of the house, anyway—the left half opened, and a balding, grey-haired man stepped out. His crisp black suit and stiff bowtie were a stark contrast to the warm smile spreading across his face.

"Ah, Ms. Neill, Mr. Munro," he said, his tone matching his smile. "Such a pleasure to finally meet you both. Ah, and you've brought a friend."

I blinked, completely taken aback by his knowledge of who we were. There was only the slightest hint of *otherness* about him, that unique ability I had that identified Community members. He wasn't a mage, but this man was definitely a human who'd been given something to extend his life.

Octavia must have done some digging on Kit's friends.

Before I had a chance to ask, he continued, "I'm Walter Whitmore, Chief of Staff at Parker House. If you'll follow me, Lady Octavia is waiting in the drawing room." He turned and stepped back inside.

I raised my eyebrows at his back, catching a matching expression from Thane. Drawing rooms were something I saw on shows like Downton Abbey, not in real life and not in the modern-day United States. I had a suspicion that Chief of Staff was a fancy way of saying butler.

But then again, we were dealing with a witch who'd been alive for at least two centuries. I'd never asked Kit how old her parents were. I never really cared before because they were both giant assholes, but now I was curious how long her mother had owned this particular mansion. Maybe Octavia had it built when drawing rooms and butlers were all the rage.

We followed Walter across the threshold and down the right wing, following a black and white checkered hallway.

What I knew of Kit's parents and family was surface level. I had learned early on in our friendship that Kit didn't like talking about them, and my attempts at prying had ended in the silent treatment. I knew she had grown up with a mostly single mother since her father had left before Kit was six. He had started a new family somewhere in Europe.

Apparently, he was "too big a deal" in the witch and warlock covens to settle for just one woman and one child. The coven leaders expected them to be grateful for the *prestige* of sharing his last name and, in Kit's case, his genetics.

Cue my giant eye roll.

In my opinion, he was just a plain old asshat who had abandoned his family when he got bored.

His absence didn't matter, though. Kit's mother had more than enough wealth in her family to provide for a daughter, and then some. Where it all came from, I hadn't a clue.

Growing up, Kit had everything she could ever need or want at her beck and call. Yet her mother couldn't provide her with the most basic need of them all—love.

All the doors in this hallway—and there were at least a dozen—were closed except one on the right. Walter led us inside.

A giant red rug covered the majority of the same black and white tiled floor, on which stood several pairs of tufted couches and coffee tables. Oversized framed portraits and paintings lined the walls, and a grand piano took up an entire corner and overlooked the massive lawn out front.

A woman with slightly greying black hair sat on one of the couches, facing us. She'd straightened her hair and styled it to curl beautifully around her shoulders and frame the skin of her face. Like Kit, she had a smooth complexion, free of any markings and that perfect shade of brown reminiscent of an espresso shot's rich foam.

Unlike Kit, her makeup was immaculate, down to the deep burgundy lipstick. She wore a collared, white and blue striped t-shirt dress cinched at the waist with a matching belt. Comfortable yet insanely expensive sandals adorned her feet and displayed the dark red pedicure that matched her lipstick. Besides a jeweled ring on a middle finger, she wore no other jewelry or signs of wealth.

She didn't need any—her entire demeanor screamed old money. Fancy country clubs probably tripped over themselves to win her membership.

"Lady Octavia, your guests have arrived," the butler said, bowing slightly and ushering us further inside.

"Thank you, Walt. Please have Shirley send in some wine," Octavia said, smiling at the man like an old friend.

"Oh, we're not here for drinks," I protested.

"Nonsense." Her sharp, hawk-like gaze met mine as Walter bowed again and slipped from the room. "You must always let your hostess take care of her guests. You're in my house, so we play by my rules."

Oi. This was not going to be easy.

"Sit." Her voice was commanding and wouldn't take no for an answer.

Luckily for her, I was getting tired and ready to sit anyway. So I did. The cream-colored couch was much more comfortable than I expected, and I had to resist the temptation to sink into its tufted fluffiness. A nap would be awesome right about now.

Thane sat beside me while Lena stood just behind the couch near my shoulder.

"I appreciate your hospitality," I said, "but time is not on our side right now."

Her sharp brown gaze flicked to Thane and Lena. "I see."

The door opened. A young woman pushed a bar cart in. She'd pulled her blonde hair into a sleek, tight bun at the nape of her neck, and she wore a well-pressed black pantsuit. Four wine glasses and two bottles of white wine stood on top of the cart.

"Ah, perfect timing, as usual, Shirley," Octavia said as the woman stopped beside our chairs.

Shirley gave a brief, stiff smile in return, then poured wine into the glasses, emptying the first bottle. She handed one to each of us.

"Thank you," I said as I took mine, our fingers brushing against each other.

The moment that our skin connected, I sensed her otherness. I tilted my head to the side as I peered at her, trying to figure out what she was. She didn't seem very witchy, but she wasn't a human with an expanded lifespan like Walter.

Her brown eyes widened, and she gave a tiny shake of her head. Her back was to her mistress.

An unsettled feeling crept into my stomach, and my shoulders tensed.

"That will be all," Octavia's sharp voice rang out. "Thank you, Shirley."

The maid gave a quick bow and backed the cart away, a slight tremor in her hands as she gripped the cart's handle.

What the fuck was that about?

I turned my attention back to Octavia to find her staring at me as a falcon would stare at a mouse. A look I knew well.

I smiled and raised my wine glass. Whatever had happened, Shirley didn't want me to mention it. "Thank you for your hospitality."

After we all took a sip of the crisp Chardonnay and commented on the delightful flavor, smell, or mouthfeel of the selection, I decided it was time to get this show on the road.

Except Octavia beat me to it.

"How is my daughter?" she asked, reclining slightly against a pillow and crossing her ankles.

What I wanted to say was inappropriate for most social circles. Kit's mom, the woman sitting in front of me, had been an unusually cold and cruel mother figure. Not a good role model for anyone.

I also wanted to tell her how Kit was really doing, besides the most recent development, of course, how she'd turned into the most amazing woman despite the horrible upbringing and with no thanks to Octavia. I wanted to tell her about the engagement with Angela, and why I thought they were perfect for each other, and how happy I was that they wouldn't invite Octavia to the wedding.

I wanted to tell her to fuck right off.

Instead of saying any of those things that she likely already knew, I looked her straight in the eyes, knowing she could read the hatred in my gaze. "Well, she's in a bit of a pickle."

Thane chuckled, likely from my severe understatement. He collapsed into a coughing fit, only this time he was prepared with the small napkin Shirley had provided us. When he pulled it away from his lips, bright red stained the once white fabric.

Octavia narrowed her eyes at him. "A reaper who chooses his final death?"

He folded the napkin to cover the stain. "Not exactly."

A sharp intake of breath came from behind us. I turned to look at Shirley, who was waiting at the back of the room with the other wine bottle. The girl's eyes had gone round, her face drained of color, and she visibly swallowed.

"Dear me." Octavia clucked her tongue. She leaned slightly to the side to glance behind me. "Am I going to have to ask you to leave?"

Shirley shook her head, but her grip on the cart's handle tightened. The metal dented.

What the fuck was happening?

"Are you okay?" With my gaze glued to Shirley, I set my glass down and stood.

The maid closed her eyes and gave a quick jerk of her head that I assumed was supposed to be a nod. A tear slipped down her cheek, leaving a red streak in its wake.

Bloody tears…

Wait. She was a fucking vampire?

Working for a witch?

I whirled on Octavia. "What the fuck is going on here?"

The woman's smile was far from inviting and warm. "Shirley is on a strict diet right now due to an unfortunate and grievous act I happened upon with our late gardener. She thanks me every day for sparing her immortal and previously useless life, don't you, Shirley?"

The vampire nodded stiffly, keeping her eyes scrunched shut. Throbbing blue veins stood out beneath her skin.

"You may go, Shirley." Octavia took a sip of her wine as if nothing was out of the ordinary here. She looked at me from behind the rim of her glass. "The reaper's blood is quite potent. We don't want to torture the poor girl, do we?"

This woman was beyond abhorrent. As much as I hated vampires, I hated this woman more.

I turned to Shirley as she wheeled the cart toward the open door. "Are you sure you're okay?"

Not a peep or even a glance before she shut the door behind her.

"Don't bother trying to get a response." Octavia swirled the wine in her glass. "I cut out her tongue."

CHAPTER 14

Monday Night

The witch's words cut through my middle like a cold blade. "You *what?* Why in sweet Mokosh's name would you do that?"

Octavia's lips twitched like she found my question funny. As if questioning the reason behind cutting out someone's tongue was the joke du jour.

"Certainly not in Mokosh's name. The girl had a rotten mouth on her. Too much talking back." She raised her glass to her deep red lips and took another sip. "Please understand. She had plenty of warning."

Warning or not, that was fucked up.

Thane's expression was grim as he regarded her. "Was your choice of punishment cleared through the agency?"

I forced myself to sit beside him again. The warmth of his presence washed over me, calming my anger enough not to murder the witch on the spot. But just barely.

Her gaze flicked to him, and she smiled. "The agency does not have any authority over what punishments I choose to inflict upon Shirley."

Thane's expression darkened further, a storm brewing beneath his otherwise calm exterior. "That is incorrect. Article 51 states any permanent form of corporal punishment must be submitted as a request to the nearest local agency and approved. That goes for anyone working—"

Octavia's short, humorless laugh cut him off. "Oh, you silly man. I've known the rules far longer than you've been alive and deceased. She doesn't *work* for me. She's indebted to me."

Thane's shoulders shook as he attempted to suppress another cough. As much as I hated watching his body breaking down this way, I was glad for the momentary interruption. I was having a really hard time coming to terms with the fact that a vampire worked for a witch, especially one of Octavia's age and distinction.

Except it wasn't as simple as that.

From the sound of it, Shirley didn't have a choice in her place of employment. Being indebted to Octavia meant normal agency rules didn't apply to the witch. She could do whatever she wanted to the girl.

How the hell did the bloodsucker get herself into this mess?

As much as I wanted to find out more and even consider helping the vampire girl—who was much older than I was based on how human she looked—I was here for one thing, and one thing only.

I gritted my teeth. "It just so happens we're here on behalf of the European Vampire Association."

"Katherine should know better than getting mixed up with the EVA," Octavia said, her upper lip curling with a sneer. "But I suppose her getting mixed up is why you're here."

Thane's cough finally subsided, leaving him winded. Leaning back against the couch, he caught his breath, and his shoulders slumped. His hard gaze remained fixed on Octavia. He wasn't going to let the tongue thing go once he returned to Miami.

I nodded. "The king and queen have requested the *scatola del cuore* you have in exchange for Kit's life."

The witch's face danced with amusement. "I may be miles away from my daughter, but I know what happened in Miami with that fae necromancer. The magical echoes she produced were quite loud."

I didn't want to ruin my chances of success by pointing out she was more than miles away; she was years away from her daughter. Decades. Lightyears, even. Kit hated her mother with a passion, and now I saw why for myself.

"Katherine should have no trouble getting herself out of harm's way," Octavia continued and finished her wine. "She needs to stop trying to hide who she is."

And now to drop the bomb.

"She can't," I said. "She bound her magic."

The wine glass shattered in the witch's hands, shards spraying out around her.

I ducked instinctively, and both Thane and Lena's arms moved across me to block the attack.

But the broken glass whirled around Octavia, spinning in a vicious tornado-like wind. The woman's face distorted, becoming as sharp and ready to murder as the fractured glass. A heartbeat later, the pieces reformed in her hand as if they'd never broken. Even the last droplet of wine had returned to its rightful place.

Goosebumps crawled across my skin. This woman was insanely powerful. I slowly realized there might be one more witch as powerful as Kit, if not more so.

Lena removed her arm from in front of me and muttered something in Yazyk under her breath.

Taking my hand in his, Thane gripped it tight. He held his body tense and narrowed his eyes at the witch as if expecting a real attack any moment.

Octavia leaned forward and placed the seamless glass on the table, her expression a fierce storm waiting to explode again. Her voice, on the other hand, was quiet and maintained perfect control. "She did what?"

The question had to be rhetorical. "So, as you can see, a pickle."

Every shred of anger wiped from Octavia's face, replaced with a calmness I'd never expect after that fury-filled display of power. She smiled and relaxed against the couch. "A pickle indeed. Very well. I will give you their precious heart box."

Thane's grip on my hand loosened slightly.

I wanted to sigh in relief, but I knew what was coming next.

"Nothing in this life is free, however," she warned.

In my life, nothing ever was. "Not even to save your daughter's life?"

She chuckled. "My Katherine chose her fate. If I'm going to help her out of this *pickle*, then she needs to thank me."

I opened my mouth to protest, knowing Kit would rather die than do—wait, a thank you? If that's all it took, then I'd force her phone into her hand and—

"In person," Octavia added, giving me a knowing look.

Well, fuck.

I glanced at Thane, who continued to study the witch carefully. The decision was up to me.

"Okay. Deal," I said.

Octavia smiled and leaned forward, holding out a hand. And here I thought I was the only one who shook on a deal to seal it.

I let go of Thane's hand and gripped hers. A sharp pain shot through my palm, and I gasped. I tried to pull back, but she held me in a death grip.

Steel slid from its sheath behind me and flashed in my periphery. Lena growled and slipped around the couch with her knives held ready to slice the witch into ribbons.

Octavia's eyes glittered with dark amusement. "Bound by blood. Surely you can understand my distrust in someone like you."

"Release her hand." Thane's command was harsh and angry. His t-port device was in his hand, already extending into the scythe. "This is completely unnecessary."

"Is it?" Octavia's gaze didn't leave mine.

I glared at the witch and waved Lena and Thane back with my free hand. "I'm not a thief anymore."

"So you say."

Crimson wisps snaked out from between our palms and swirled around our clasped hands, binding them together. As the magic sank into our skin, tingles spread from my fingers, up my arm, and wrapped around my heart with a quick squeeze.

"If you wanted a blood oath, you could have just asked nicely," I said through clenched teeth.

Even if I had wanted to accidentally yet conveniently "forget" our agreement, now I had no choice. Failing to honor the blood oath with a witch this powerful would no doubt result in some horrible outcome, probably lifetime indentured servitude like Shirley.

I would be sure to leave that part out when I told Kit. Telling her would definitely result in a horrible outcome.

Revealing my royal status to Octavia might have helped, but I also didn't want to reveal that card just yet. Knowledge could be power, and I might need all the leverage I could get with this crazy lady later.

"I could have just asked, yes," she said plainly and let go.

I inspected my hand. Only a drop of blood smeared across my palm. I accepted a napkin from Thane and pressed it against my palm. I should have just wiped it on her fancy couch as a reminder of who she was dealing with—a desperate woman not above petty actions.

"You are on thin ice," Thane warned her, retracting his scythe but keeping the device out.

She regarded him with a smile.

Behind us, the door opened and Walter strode in, carrying a small item wrapped in cloth. He placed the package on the table between us.

A ghost must have walked over my grave. The chill seeping through me almost stung.

Judging by the speed with which he'd arrived and with no obvious communication from the lady of the house, she knew we were coming. She knew exactly what we came for, and she was prepared to give it up. The deal we made was just an added bonus.

Fuck. She totally played me.

"Thank you, Walt." Octavia gestured to the bundle. "All yours."

Thane picked it up and unwrapped the cloth. A shiny silver box a little bigger than his fist sat within, a heart etched into the metal lid. The only other marking on the entire box was a keyhole.

Thane attempted to lift the lid, but it didn't open. "I can sense the magic enclosing the box. Is there a key?"

"Bianca has it," Octavia said.

I blinked at her. "You took the box without the key?"

She chuckled. "No amount of magic would keep me from opening it if I wanted to."

A shiver ran up my spine. I needed to do some digging on this woman, and now this damn box was piquing my interest even more.

What the hell was inside?

Whatever it was, it better not get me in trouble like the last box. Time to get the fuck out of here.

We stood, my tired body trying to resist each movement.

Thane flipped the cloth back over the box and activated his teleportation device. Even if I wanted to steal the device and fly back to Italy, forcing Thane to return to Miami via cab or plane, I couldn't. My limbs felt like boulders.

But after we got back home, that was it—no more teleporting.

"Tell Katherine I'm looking forward to her visit," the witch said, not bothering to stand. Her gaze sharpened on me. "I expect to see her before the next full moon."

I rolled my eyes as the floor vanished beneath us.

What was it with witches and werewolves always following the moon's cycle? Like I even knew when the full moon occurred. Kit would, at least, and there was always Google. Hopefully we had a bit of time before she had to face this monster because I would absolutely be going with her.

When the world reappeared from the dark void, we were back in the EVA's Italian villa. The single vampire guard posted outside the throne room didn't even blink an eye as we rematerialized right in front of him.

He moved to open the door, gesturing us inside.

Talk about service. Of course, we *had* just returned with an item they sought and probably never would have gotten their filthy clawed hands on without our help.

Sure enough, the leaders of the EVA sat on their crimson thrones, waiting for us.

CHAPTER 15

Tuesday Early Morning

Vincenzo sat like a block of expertly sculpted ice, his dark brown eyes the only part of him moving as he tracked our approach. The queen, on the other hand, couldn't contain her excitement.

Bianca leaned forward, gripping the arms of her chair. Her red lips parted eagerly. "Is that it?"

Thane unwrapped the bundle and held up the heart box. "As requested."

A female vampire who'd been standing behind her came down the dais steps and took the box. She deposited it into the queen's outstretched palms.

Bianca ran a hand over the lid delicately, as if it were a precious pet. "We thought for sure she'd let her daughter die before returning this."

I raised an eyebrow, hating this woman even more now. "You sent us thinking we'd fail? Why?"

"Very few things bring us pleasure anymore." Her gaze flicked to mine. Unchecked hatred flashed through her brown eyes. "Watching that witch burn would have been very pleasurable."

"Sorry to disappoint you," I said flatly.

The queen set the box on her lap and opened the lid. The sickly sweet scent of rusting metal quickly filled the room. The few vampires in attendance didn't move, but I caught more than one flared nostril. She had trained her undead fiends well.

Dipping her hands in gently, the queen removed the item from within the box. Fresh blood dripped down her arms as she raised the thing to her face.

That thing turned out to be a beating heart.

How the fuck was it still beating?

Bile rose in the back of my throat, burning its way up. I swallowed hard.

"Our beloved Fortunato has returned to us," her voice rang out, echoing through the vast room.

My eyebrows crept toward my hairline. I knew vampires could withstand some wounds most others found fatal—except for a stake to the heart, decapitation, or fire, of course—but this? Living without a body? I'd never heard of it.

I leaned toward Thane and whispered, "Did you know they could do that? The whole heart thing?"

He nodded. "Only with the *veteres*."

I thought I knew a lot about vampires, but it turned out there was still more to learn. "The what?"

"The original vampiric creations of a necromancer," he explained quietly. "They're the strongest of their kind because of the undiluted lineage."

My jaw dropped open, and I almost forgot to whisper. "A necromancer created vampires? Why?"

He glanced at me and grinned. "Growing up a badass didn't include studying?"

I snorted softly. "School and studying weren't exactly my strong suits."

"Fair point. The necromancer created vampires trying to cure a virus. It worked, a little too well."

No wonder Maddox had always enjoyed studying the Community. This stuff was fascinating—such a shame I hadn't paid more attention earlier in life.

"How many of these *veteres* are there?"

"Still walking?" He thought for a moment. "Maybe three. The practice of saving their hearts when they finished with the world started a few centuries ago. This is one of six."

"Why the hell do they do it? Why not just die, like, all the way?" I whispered, glancing at the king and queen. Both were too busy inspecting the beating heart to care about our conversation.

"Their blood is used whenever they crown a new king or queen," he explained. "They gain strength and knowledge from ingesting it. Or so they claim."

I shuddered. "Gross. How did Octavia get her hands on this one?"

"I'm not sure I even want to know."

Me neither. I certainly didn't want to know *why* she wanted it either. Some things were just better not knowing. Although, I did wonder if it involved Shirley, the vampire without a tongue.

"Time to uphold your part of the bargain," I called up to the royal pair.

The queen set the heart back into place, stroked it like a beloved pet one last time, and closed the lid. She slid one of her blood-soaked fingers into her mouth, closing her eyes and moaning as she sucked the blood from her skin.

My lips curled in disgust, and Lena made a gagging sound behind me.

Vincenzo's dark brown eyes burned red, a sign of his telepathic communication with his minions.

Ignoring the hungry slurping from the queen turned out to be much harder than I would have liked, so I breathed a huge sigh of relief when two ugly vampires entered the room from a side door. Kit was between them.

As the vamps removed her chains with jerky movements, her confused glance turned toward us. Her mouth and eyes popped open wide. "She gave it to you?"

There goes someone underestimating me again. I thought we'd moved past that. "Why does everyone doubt me?"

Thane smirked. His face contorted, and he fell into another coughing fit. Blood splattered the floor before he could get a tissue up to his mouth. He was getting worse fast.

"What did you promise her?" Kit asked, rubbing the red marks around her wrists as she approached.

"Nothing terrible," I said, rubbing the reaper's back as

he continued to hack up a lung. Thankfully not literally. There wasn't much else I could do for him. "She just wants you to say thank you in person by the next full moon. Such a narcissist, right?"

She gaped at me, her face draining of color. "You agreed to that?"

"Of course I did." I glared at her. "Time isn't exactly on our side here."

"I told you her requests come with dire consequences."

I rolled my eyes. "You're being dramatic. Seeing your mom is unpleasant, not dire."

She closed her eyes and breathed deeply. "You have no idea what you've just done."

"Enlighten me."

Opening her eyes again, she focused them on me. "Bound as I am, she'll have me under her control within seconds of stepping foot in her home."

"So get with Angela and unbind yourself," I said, an angry flush rising up my neck. "You shouldn't have done it to begin with. This is the only thing I agree with your mother on. Embrace who you are, for fuck's sake. Learn to control it."

"You don't understand—"

"You're right. I don't," I snapped. "But what concerns me right now is tracking down the dragonstone. Everything else will have to wait."

Thane cleared his throat and tucked the bloody tissue away. Sweat glistened across his forehead.

The vampire queen's grotesque sucking stopped, and her eyes snapped open. "The dragonstone?"

Oh, I could just kick myself sometimes.

Gritting my teeth, I nodded. "You've heard of it?"

"Of course. Such a small world." Her blood-stained lips pulled up into a devious smile. "We know where it is."

Thane drew a sharp breath and slipped his hand into mine, entwining our fingers.

My heart lurched to a stop. I could hardly breathe. "Where?"

"We have it here in the villa," Bianca said casually, licking one last drop of blood from her finger.

Oh. My. Gods.

I squeezed Thane's hand until my knuckles turned white. "It belongs to me."

She raised an eyebrow. "Is that so? Then why is it in our possession?"

"It was stolen."

"Such a pity," she said. "Now it's ours."

Arguing with her would be a lost cause. I had no way of proving the dragonstone belonged to me. My stomach churned painfully.

"Not for much longer," the king added.

I frowned. "Who bought it?"

"No one. As you may recall, we vampires enjoy collecting rare and invaluable items." Vincenzo's eyes glinted dangerously. "The stone will be awarded as the grand prize of the next Blood Trials."

I recalled that fact very clearly, considering I'd almost found myself included in Xavier's collection. "I'll buy it."

Bianca laughed. "It's not for sale. Money is not something we need or want."

"I'm sure there's something you must want, like that heart," I pressed. "Something else found only in Mirognya."

She licked another streak of red from her fingers. "We're afraid not."

There was no way in hell that was true. I was sure there was something out there that would interest them enough to be persuaded. But how was I going to figure that out in time to save Thane?

I glanced down at our joined hands.

An insane idea gripped me.

"Then I'll fight in the Blood Trials," I said. "I'll fight for it."

Thane's hand tightened on mine, and Kit took a startled step back.

"I have no idea what that is," Lena said right behind me, her voice hard, "but it's not happening."

Bianca smiled. "Your little warrior is right. The trials are for those interested in joining our way of life and those looking to ascend the immortal ladder. Of which you are neither."

"What better way to test recruits than to pit them against a real enemy?" I challenged.

"Veronica, no," Thane said, turning me to face him. "You've had some crazy ideas, but this one tops them all."

"We don't have any other options." I pleaded for understanding and acceptance with my gaze. "I can't lose you."

He reached a hand up and stroked my cheek. "And I can't lose *you*, you stubborn phoenix. We'll find another way."

I wanted to believe him, to believe that there was another way. Pessimism didn't come naturally to me, but even I could admit there were no other options.

Deep down, I knew this was the only way.

Why else would the gods have led us here?

I shook my head and turned to the king. "Let me fight. Please."

The queen sneered. "It is forbidden."

Vincenzo held up a hand to silence us all, his jeweled rings scattering rainbows along the walls. He considered me for a moment. Unlike his queen, whatever thoughts the king had, they didn't show.

"Let her appeal to the royal conclave," he said at last.

Bianca whirled toward her husband and hissed. "You would invite an outsider to the conclave?"

"We're sure they will find the distraction as entertaining as we will," he said.

"When and where?" I asked before she could come up with another excuse.

"V, you can't be serious," Kit said, her dark brown eyes full of concern.

"I've never been more serious."

"It's settled then. The next conclave will be held here in Rome two evenings from now," Vincenzo said, rising from his throne and buttoning his suit jacket. "Now, if you'll excuse us, dawn approaches."

Sunlight didn't kill vampires outright, but it definitely weakened them. Plus, even vampires needed rest from time to time, and as a nocturnal species, daytime meant sleep. I had a hunch this was less an issue with the sun and more a diplomatic way of kicking us out.

"I'll be there," I said and followed the others out of the throne room.

When the door shut behind us, Kit spun around and

slapped me upside the head. "Are you insane? Did becoming a queen scramble your common sense?"

Wincing, I rubbed at my head and looked expectantly toward Lena.

The warrior woman raised her hands, which were remarkably free of weapons. "I'm with her on this one. It was for your own good."

"Make that three of us," Thane said, removing the teleportation device from his pocket.

"Insane or not, this is our only option." I placed my hands on my hips. "Why am I the only one who can see that?"

Lena rolled her eyes. "Because the rest of us aren't batshit crazy. As Thane said, we'll find another option."

The reaper activated the black circle and took my hand.

"Until another idea presents itself, I'm sticking with this one," I said, taking Lena's hand.

She took Kit's in her free hand.

Just before the floor fell away, Kit muttered, "Are you sure you're not a dodo bird?"

When the world reappeared, we were in Adam's office. A giant mahogany desk took up the back of the room, and equally massive bookshelves spread across the entire wall opposite floor-to-ceiling windows.

The archangel sat behind his desk, his pristine white wings folded against his back. He rested his elbows on the arms of his chair and teepeed his hands in front of his face. His blue eyes flicked toward us, and a look of relief passed over his otherwise angelic expression for the briefest of moments.

Someone argued vehemently in the chair before him.

That someone turned to look at who had interrupted his tirade and made me completely forget Kit's last question. Colin.

CHAPTER 16

Monday Night

The last time I'd seen the fae man, Kit's magic had impaled him on the conference room wall. Thane and I had helped him down right before I followed William, the necromancer, through the portal to Mirognya.

A lot had happened since then.

Colin's auburn hair, reminiscent of autumn leaves, glittered even in the office's limited light. His skin was the color of fresh milk, except the slightest hint of gold ran through his veins. Like all the fae, he was more handsome than most humans.

Tonight, he wore a more business-like outfit than I'd seen on him before: a black blazer over a red button-down shirt, black tie, and black slacks.

Blue-green eyes that shifted color as he moved opened wide as they landed on me. He leaped to his feet. "Veronica! You're safe!"

"That makes two of us." I wanted to smile, but the adrenaline from all that had occurred with the vampires was wearing off fast. My cheeks quivered with my pitiful attempt.

He chuckled as he came toward me, arms out for a hug. "Why am I not surprised to hear that coming from you?"

I accepted the hug, though it felt awkward, like he thought we were better friends than we were. Technically, I hardly knew the guy, though he'd always been much friendlier than I'd ever expected a fae to be. He was an anomaly.

"Good to see you." When we parted, I faced Adam. "I'm going to ask the Royal Conclave for their permission to fight in the Blood Trials."

You could have heard a pin drop. Then everyone started arguing and yelling at once.

"That's absurd!" Colin shouted.

Adam pinched the bridge of his nose. "Who let her think that was a good idea?"

"We've already discussed it, and the answer is no," Thane said.

I let them argue it out as if I wasn't there, fatigue weighing me down and keeping me quiet.

"What in Dazhbog's name did I miss?" Ivan's voice whispered in my ear. He picked a hell of a time to return from Mirfeniksa.

I chuckled and explained the series of events in as few words as possible, yawning partway through. At some point,

Lena realized the other phoenix had arrived.

"Ivan!" she shouted, flailing her arms around in an impressive display of exasperation. "Please tell your tsarina that she is *not* going to fight vampires. One of us will be her champion instead if we have to."

The others noticed Ivan's arrival for the first time, and the arguing ceased.

Thane blew out a breath and sat in one of the empty chairs. His heavy-lidded eyes looked as exhausted as I felt. "Find anything on the stone that can help us out of this predicament?"

"Sadly, no," Ivan sighed. "Mama Anya knew about the same as I did. I also had to keep avoiding Pietr, who was trying to pin me down with questions. He suspects we're up to something. But Lena's right, V. One of us will fight in your place."

I shook my head, and the world spun, forcing me to close my eyes for a moment. When was the last time I had gotten any sleep? Any of us, for that matter. All the time zone hopping had me turned around to the point I wasn't even sure what day it was anymore.

"If the vampires allow us to fight for the stone, I can guarantee they won't let anyone but me, or maybe Thane, fight," I said.

I didn't know everything about vampires, but this was a given. It would be hard enough getting the conclave to agree in the first place, and they would only accept the most challenging or most entertaining fighter—me.

"Then Thane will fight," Lena said, giving him an apologetic shrug. "No offense, but it's his life we're fighting for anyway."

I opened my eyes and gazed at him, my shoulders slumping. His expression darkened with understanding.

The reaper's voice was as grim as his face, "I won't be able to fight at the rate my body's breaking down. I won't be able to do much of anything soon."

"Are you even aware of what occurs at the Blood Trials?" Colin asked.

"Let me guess, a lot of blood is spilled?" I asked, rubbing my temples where a throb had started to build.

I couldn't remember the last time I'd had a headache. All that magic training in Mirfeniksa must have helped keep them at bay. Too bad it hadn't helped with stress.

"Seriously, V?" Kit shook her head.

I shrugged. "Someone's got to lighten the mood."

"They're more brutal than you could ever imagine," the fae man said. "There are four trials, each getting progressively harder than the last. Sometimes they fight in large groups, sometimes one against one. As impressive as your fighting skills are, you don't have the killer instinct to do what must be done."

When the lives of the people I loved were at stake, I could rip someone apart. He should know that about me by now, if nothing else. "My magic is stronger now—"

He held up a hand and shook his head. "No magic is permitted within the trials."

Well, fuck. I did not see that coming.

Not using magic didn't change anything. If I lost, Thane would die. If I didn't fight, Thane would die, and there was no way I would be able to live with myself. Waiting around and doing nothing was not going to happen. I would fight for his life or die trying.

"*I'm* stronger now, and I have no problem killing those filthy bloodsuckers," I said.

"Some of them won't be vampires yet," Colin said.

Gods, he was such a buzzkill. How did he even know all of this?

"People who choose to become vampires are just as bad," I said, more harshly than I intended. I took a deep breath. "While I appreciate your insight, let it go. I'm fighting."

The room tilted, and I grabbed onto the back of a chair for support. Several sets of arms grabbed for me at once, and I couldn't help but laugh.

"I'm just tired," I explained, brushing all but one set of arms away. I leaned into Thane's warmth and inhaled the sweet scent that always accompanied him. "Let's finish this discussion later after a well-deserved nap."

Thank the gods, no one argued.

"Can I speak with you for a moment before you go?" Colin asked, his gaze drifting to Thane briefly. "Alone?"

"Sure," I said. After extracting myself from the reaper's arms, I squeezed his hand once before letting go.

Thane kissed my forehead and moved toward Adam, where the two immediately started a discussion on agency matters. Hopefully, he would tell the archangel about the tongueless vampire, Shirley.

Waving away Lena and Ivan as they tried to follow, I accompanied the fae man out into the empty reception area.

Either Adam's receptionist didn't work this late, or she was on a break. I still didn't know why the archangel bothered to have a reception area—his was the only office up here.

A tan leather couch sat along the wall on our left, and a few matching chairs faced each other on the right. Both seating areas were complete with glass-top coffee tables, holding various magazines from the last several decades. Besides the furniture, a few potted trees, and the elevator, the room was barren.

Colin turned to face me and ran a hand through his auburn hair. "I'm sorry for the distance before you left. I hope you know I hold you in the highest regard."

I smiled. "I appreciate that, but no hard feelings. For real."

He took my hand and stroked the back of it. "Can I make it up to you over dinner before you throw yourself head first into harm's way again?"

Oh, shit. Was he asking me out on a date? I thought I'd been pretty obvious about my status with Thane.

I removed my hand from his. "That sounds lovely, but I'm afraid I've given you the wrong idea. I'm not available for a date."

Colin narrowed his eyes. "Don't tell me you've settled for the reaper."

I smirked. Jealousy was not a good look for him. "I wouldn't say settled, but yes, he's my mate."

Surprise never looked as genuine as it did now on his face. "*Mate?*"

Pulling down the top of my dirt-stained tank top revealed the red bonded mark that resembled a falcon in flight. "It's a thing in my world. Our souls chose each other."

His face flushed red, and he pressed his lips together tightly. "You've made a mistake."

I raised an eyebrow. What an odd response. "Tell me something I don't know. But it's too late now."

"Is it?" He took both my hands this time, gripping mine a bit too tight to feel nice. "Can it be broken?"

Glaring at him, I wrenched my hands free. So much for him being a rare friendly fae. This line of questioning only pissed me off.

"Even if I wanted to, which I definitely do not, no. It can't. Good night, Colin."

"Veronica, wait." He grabbed my arm, pinching my skin painfully.

Nope.

I lit my arm on fire, and he snatched his smoking hand away.

"Don't touch me again. You're lucky my warriors weren't here to see that," I warned.

"Your warriors?"

"Turns out I'm a queen." I opened the door to the office and left the fae man gaping behind me.

After a hot yet far too quick shower, I slept like the dead through most of Tuesday and almost into Wednesday. When the dead were left alone to rest peacefully instead of being brought back to a half-life status by some maniacal necromancer, that is.

In Wednesday's pre-dawn hours, I paced my penthouse apartment, blissfully alone for the first time in what felt like forever.

Well, it was as close to private as I was going to get.

Thane sprawled across my bed sound asleep while Lena and Ivan shared my guest room. Two angels still stood guard on the outside terrace.

Even though I'd been practically swaying on my feet in Adam's office, I'd pulled Kit aside to apologize before she left. The last thing I wanted to do was put her in a bad situation with her mom, or with Angela. I didn't realize how serious her warning about making a deal with her mom had been.

My bestie wasn't going to let me off the hook that easily. She needed time to cool off, which I understood.

I hadn't known what visiting her mother would mean for her, and I still didn't quite understand what she meant when she said her mom would have Kit under her control. It didn't sound good, but I was also pretty sure most people felt that way about their controlling mothers.

I was confident Kit would put Octavia in her place even without her full powers.

That's what I kept telling myself anyway—one problem at a time.

By the time everyone else woke, Miami dawn had arrived in all her glory. Bands of golden light stretched out across the ocean waves far below the penthouse terrace. Seagulls cawed and dove into the water, rising once they caught their breakfast.

As I leaned against the railing, breathing in the salty air, warm arms wrapped around my waist. I smiled and leaned back against him.

"I could get used to this sight," Thane murmured, his breath tickling my ear.

"Gorgeous, isn't it?"

"I meant you in those shorts." He pressed his very obvious aroused state against my butt. "Your ass looks amazing."

I laughed, wishing for all the world that this was our life. Playful banter, amazing sex, and no impending death looming over our heads. I turned in his embrace to face him, wrapping my arms around his neck and pressing my lips to his.

A glorious burn rippled through me, growing in intensity as he pulled me closer to him and deepened the kiss. The mark on my chest blazed with a similar heat as his erection pressed against me again. My body throbbed with desire.

Someone cleared their throat behind us. Someone who deserved a beating for the interruption.

For fuck's sake.

We didn't stop immediately but slowed the kiss until just our foreheads touched. What I wouldn't give just to have Thane all to myself.

No distractions.

Forever.

When we finally separated, I glared at the intruder. "Yes?"

Dressed in a fluffy, white bathrobe and matching slippers, Lena held up a bowl filled with a heaping amount of rainbow-hued cereal. She crunched happily. "This is amazing, but you're out of milk, and I'm going to need more."

I groaned, but Thane just smirked. He kissed me on the nose and drew his t-port device.

"I'll be right back." He blinked out of sight before I could stop him.

The last thing I wanted was to worsen his condition by teleporting, especially for something so trivial as cereal. I had completely forgotten about talking to him last night when we came to my penthouse, but I intended to put an end to it.

No more teleporting.

"Really, Lena?" I smoothed back my hair, still feeling his touch on my skin.

Her expression looked innocent. Almost.

"What?"

CHAPTER 17

Thursday Evening

We spent most of Wednesday and Thursday preparing for the vampires' conclave. From what Adam had told us, the kings and queens of the six global vampire associations met with their Master Vampires and Vampiresses at separate conclaves once a quarter. They always held trials soon after to take advantage of all the association's leaders gathered in one place.

Had I known that one day I would need to fight vampires to save the love of my life, I would have flown over the North American Vampire Association's building to gather some intel. The current American king and queen lived outside of Washington, D.C., so they usually held meetings and trials there. I could have made a lot of money selling those secrets.

Hell, I would have done it just for fun if I didn't live so far away.

Conclaves were the equivalent of royal balls, which meant I needed a gown. Shopping with Lena had almost turned into a disaster since she refused to wear anything I picked out. Everything was too "girly" or didn't move well enough for fighting.

In the end, we settled on a sleek black and white pantsuit that matched Ivan's. And by settled, I meant she won the argument. I had to admit, she looked hot in a fitted suit and purple tie.

I also spent the last two days trying to convince Thane not to teleport anymore and let the rest of us handle it from here. There was no need for him to attend the conclave other than my own selfish reasons.

Except arguing with him was like trying to move a griffin by hand. *I* was supposed to be the stubborn one, but he refused to stay behind.

Ivan finally had the bright idea to see how his realm walking ability worked with Thane's deteriorating condition. After some jumps around the world showed no signs of affecting the reaper, they concluded it worked. We guessed it had something to do with one being a natural-born talent versus a man-made device, even if that man happened to be an angel.

Whatever the reason, I breathed a huge sigh of relief. I didn't want to leave Thane's side, even for a night. If our days were numbered, then I wanted each day to be with him.

By Thursday afternoon, I was restless and ready to get

going. I took another glance at my reflection, loving the oversized full-length mirror in my penthouse's bathroom for occasions like these. Not that there'd been too many in the past, but it came in handy tonight.

The gown I'd selected was an off-white satin halter top, gathered at the waist where the fabric met with the plunging V-neck. A little boob tape kept my ladies in place, and my back was open to the night air. I smirked at my reflection.

I certainly had a look.

Memories of the night I met Thane at the Star Island party surfaced in a rush of heat and desire. I bit my lip, wishing we could have been just two ordinary people meeting for the first time that night. That we could have spent the last few months dating, dancing, and rolling around in the sheets instead of facing one disaster after another.

Sighing, I tucked my memories away.

There was no sense dwelling on something that didn't occur and never could have occurred. Focusing on the future was the only way forward. Tonight's dress would accentuate my wings when I introduced myself—nothing like a little dramatic display to get the vampires' attention.

I had pulled my blonde hair up into a French twist, allowing a few nearly white wisps to frame my face. Amethysts and diamonds lined the three collet necklaces draped across my collarbones. I added some mascara, a few swipes of blush, and a light pink lip gloss to make my features pop.

The only thing missing tonight would be Kit, but there was no way she could come with me until the vampires lifted her banishment.

So, never.

When I entered the penthouse's living room, Thane had his back to me, and Lena was laughing at some joke Ivan had just cracked. She turned toward me, and her eyes widened.

"Hot damn!" She slapped Thane on the back. "You are one lucky man."

The reaper turned to face me, and his jaw clenched. His gaze drank me in from head to toe, and judging by the sapphire hue of his irises, he liked what he saw. He moved toward me, a sleek panther stalking his prey. The spice of cardamom curled around me with his approach.

If it was even possible, he looked just as good in tonight's navy blue suit as he did naked. The reaper's tailor cut that fabric to accentuate his tall frame and hard physique perfectly. A pale purple tie covered in grinning skulls added a very sexy touch.

He brushed my cheek with his hand, tucking a strand of hair behind my ear. Leaning close, he murmured, "I would love nothing more than to rip that dress from your perfect body and claim you as mine once again."

Instantly, fire rushed through me, my core throbbing. I was ready for him to prove it, to shred the gown, lift my legs, and claim me till sunrise.

If only his life weren't on the line.

I tilted my chin up and kissed him lightly on the lips. "You better make good on that promise once this is all over."

"I always make good on my promises," he growled against my lips. His hands moved to grip my hips, and I had to bite back a moan.

"I don't mean to ruin a good moment, but you're forgetting something," Lena called.

With a promise in my gaze to finish what we'd started later, I took a calming breath and stepped around Thane.

Lena held out my crown—the one I'd purposefully left back in Mirognya.

I scrunched up my face. "Do I have to? Don't you think the wings will be enough?"

She rolled her eyes and gestured for me to bend enough for her to place the metal circle on my head. "You sound like a child. Yes, you have to. You need to make it extremely clear that you are their equal, if not their superior."

"I'm definitely superior. I don't need a crown to prove that," I said, straightening despite the weight of the crown. Not physically, of course. "They drink blood to survive, for fuck's sake."

Ivan grinned. "Maybe keep your opinions to yourself tonight."

"I am perfectly capable of censoring myself, thank you very much." I paused. "Most of the time."

Thane offered his arm. "Shall we?"

Using Ivan's ability, we gathered in Adam's office for any last-minute tips or warnings before making the jump back to Rome. Or maybe it was forward if we went by time zones.

The archangel stood at the office's sliding glass doors, eyeing the sunset. That's what it looked like, anyway, but maybe he was praying. We could certainly use all the prayers we could get.

He turned toward us, and his bright white wings no longer covered his equally white suit. With his close-cropped sandy blond hair and blue eyes, he reminded me of Daniel Craig in his Bond days. Only with the wrong color suit and sprouting wings.

Bond had nothing on Adam tonight.

When I raised my eyebrows at the archangel's polished look, he smiled. "I will join you tonight."

"Don't trust us youngins to stay out of trouble?" I joked—kind of.

He chuckled. "I believe the vampires will appreciate an authority figure from the human world."

"I won't argue against having more backup," Thane said, and I agreed.

While I didn't expect the vampires to do anything to rock the Community boat by attacking, kidnapping, or draining us dry, I always liked to be prepared for the worst. Having Adam there in an official capacity would give us a fighting chance,

Or an eyewitness.

Although Ivan could have jumped us straight inside the vampires' Italian villa, Adam had recommended a more peaceful, less dramatic approach. Meaning he didn't want to get attacked by a horde of super powerful, bloodsucking fiends the moment we arrived.

Fair.

While he might have won the peaceful approach idea, I still wanted to make a statement. Let them know exactly how powerful we were as allies and how formidable we would be as enemies if they provoked us.

When we suddenly appeared outside the villa's front portico, a group of vampires about to enter hissed and drew back. After the initial surprise, they eyed us cautiously. Semi-dramatic effect with no bloodshed achieved.

Wins all around.

The only good thing—if there even was one—about joining a gathering of vampires of this stature was the fact that they were all old, which in vampire terms meant beautiful. Inhumanly gorgeous. Not the gangly, grotesque beings that clawed and dug their way out of their graves and made me want to gag.

Plus, the older ones wouldn't try to eat us all night. Not obviously, anyway.

No, the centuries-old men and women here tonight were practically radiant, glowing if that were at all possible. It wasn't, for the record, but if the general human population had attended this gathering, they would have shed tears at the sheer beauty of these beings. No amount of Botox or plastic surgery could recreate these masterpieces.

Unlike our last visit when we arrived at the back of the house in complete darkness, tonight, well-positioned uplighting cast long shadows along the outer walls of the Italian villa. Additional solar-powered lights led guests up the path from the main parking area at the base of the hill.

Ignoring the curious murmurings from those remaining outside, we entered the villa and met with our vampire guide. He led us down several hallways we didn't see the last time. Painted murals covered most of the walls, depicting scenes of luxury and debauchery.

History had never been my forte, but I always enjoyed the art that came with the lessons. These scenes reminded me of ancient Roman times, where everyone wore togas and lounged on chaises. The people drank and ate together, and in these images, vampires did as well.

They also had sex—lots and lots of sex.

Depictions of every pose I'd ever encountered, plus many more I hadn't, accompanied our walk to the gathering. After one fascinating scene, I glanced at Thane and grinned. He eyed the pose before turning a hungry gaze on me. His smirk lit my insides on fire.

Joining the most powerful European vampires might have been a terrible idea for my impulse control, or lack thereof.

After following the guide through two ornate doors, we stood at the top balustrade of two sweeping staircases lined with gilded rails and surveyed the large area below. Because the original owner built the back of the villa going down a slope, the room provided ample space for the official conclave. The main floor sat at the bottom of the staircases.

The black rose design used in the throne room also appeared here, embellishing the crown molding with a repeating floral pattern. Sconces were crafted into thorny black roses as well and lit the walls along the stairs. Double French doors on the three main walls opened to the night sky and the gardens beyond.

This room wasn't as long as the throne room, so only one chandelier dangled over the attendees. The multitude of bulbs still provided more than enough light for a nocturnal crowd and for us to see them.

And boy, did we see them.

I had thought Lady Emilia's way of introduction was unique.

The first and only time I'd met the Master Vampiress of Miami was to convince her of the necromancers' threat to the Community and to assist us in combating them. When Thane and I'd arrived, she was in the middle of a compromising situation—sex. She was having sex right in front of us without a care in the world, and damn if I didn't get turned on.

In my defense, anyone would have. She used her vampiric ability to heighten my body's reaction to wanton levels. Thank the gods for Thane's resistance to her *influence*. He caught me right before I took my shirt off, then I almost had sex with *him* for the first time in an alley.

Fucking vampires. Always making a mess of things.

After all that, she'd turned us down, not wanting to involve her kind in fae politics. I hadn't seen her since.

Anyway, it turned out Emilia wasn't all that unique.

Lena's breath tickled my neck as she whispered, "What was that about not having an orgy fantasy?"

Sure enough, that was what we had walked in on.

Sweaty bodies—some fully naked and some still in ball gowns and partially undone suits—draped across each other in erotic poses. Cries of passion mixed with moans and snarls. As they thrust and ground against each other, they also fed. Some drank from the vampire they fucked while others found offered wrists from nearby voyeurs.

I guessed this was their way of getting to know each other better.

Waiting for them to notice us, I swallowed against a suddenly dry mouth. My body responded to the sex in the air, growing warm and wanting Thane all over me, stretching and filling me. I bit my tongue hard enough to draw blood, trying to keep my thoughts focused on the goal. Not on sex.

Stop thinking about sex!

The gods were on our side—it didn't take long for them to notice.

Our unique scents caught the attention of those closest to us before spreading like wildfire. Bodies ceased their thrusts and grunts. Limbs untangled from others. Every head in the room turned our way, and all conversation, even the music, stopped.

It was as silent as the grave.

Yeah, I went there.

Although I couldn't smell emotions like vampires could, their bodies emitted anger at the disruption and hunger for the presumed meal like heat waves. I tightened my grip on Thane's hand but urged myself to remain calm. Fear would only excite them.

I let my wings unfurl, the flames caressing against my back. The wisps of hair around my face moved gently with the heat. Beside me, Adam allowed his wings to spread as well, though only enough for the onlookers to confirm what he was.

Despite their typically neutral demeanor and creepy ability to hide emotions, more than one gasp escaped those undead lips.

Vincenzo strode into view, his red robe hanging wide open and providing an excellent view of his toned, dancer-like body and very aroused state. He had slicked his dark brown hair back and styled his goatee into points, a look that accentuated his overly large nose.

Among all the beautiful faces tonight, you'd think that nose would be to his detriment. Instead, it set him apart in an intriguing, eye-catching way.

Beside him, Bianca's gaze smoldered as she looked me over. Maybe she thought I wouldn't come, or maybe she was pissed that my crown was bigger than hers.

Whatever it was, I was glad to see her fully dressed in a skintight, strapless black gown with a poufy mermaid bottom. Her long blonde hair fell around her shoulders, and a giant ruby hung down to dip between her breasts.

I wasn't always the jealous type, but she was beyond gorgeous, and I didn't need my man ogling her naked goods right beside me.

Vincenzo raised his chalice toward us. "We have special guests joining us this evening. It's our pleasure to introduce Adam Larue, the Death Enforcement Agency's Archangel in Miami, and Her Majesty Veronica Neill, tsarina of Mirfeniksa, the land of the phoenixes."

He let that sink into their undead, statue-like composures before introducing my friends. Once he finished, we made our way down the stairs. Thane gave my hand a gentle squeeze.

Vampires continued to unwind and detach themselves from their partners and groups. Pushing clothing back into place or remaining in the buff, they slowly gathered around their king.

The room was still eerily quiet, as if the entire vampire congregation held their non-existent collective breath.

For what, though?

The king and queen met us at the base of the stairs.

Bianca's sharp gaze moved to each of us in turn. "You smell infinitely better than the last time we saw you."

I was pretty confident that wasn't a compliment, just a statement of fact after our gravedigging escapades. Considering our surroundings—and the fact that she was right—I would let the dig slide for now.

"You're too kind," I said, smiling as Thane squeezed my hand again.

"Why have you allowed outsiders to the conclave?" a man's tenor voice called out.

The crowd moved to the side to allow the speaker forward.

Like the others, he was insanely handsome. Blond hair fell to his bare chin, and deep blue eyes narrowed shrewdly in our direction. Well-defined muscles along his arms, chest, and abs glistened beneath the chandelier. He'd lost his shirt but not his pants, though he hadn't bothered to zip those back up. A perfectly shaped V tempted the gaze below his waist.

As he looked us over, his nostrils flared, and he snapped his gaze to me. Hunger rose like a beast within him.

Thane's grip tightened, and he took a step forward possessively. But I just stared right back. I didn't cower easily.

"Thank you for bringing us to our next point, Philip," the king said, sarcasm thick in his tone. It was the only emotion I'd sensed from him since our first meeting.

"The tsarina has requested a chance to fight in the Blood Trials."

CHAPTER 18

Thursday Evening

Well, that declaration sure got the party started again. Noise erupted across the hall. Some vampires argued with each other while others leaned close and gossiped, staring our group members down.

Hunger, desire, and anger were all alive and well tonight. The desire was undeniable with all the nakedness going on.

Lena and Ivan melted away, drifting into the crowd. Their goal would be to eavesdrop on conversations, hoping to learn anything that might help me sway the conclave. Any tips on how to win the trials themselves would be like unexpected bacon in a juicy burger.

Of course, part of the goal included not getting distracted. I'd warned them about the *influence* ability. Hopefully, they remembered.

I also wanted my warriors spread out in case any vampires got a bit carried away with the whole fighting idea and tried to start the trials tonight. Having a surprise backup plan was always a good idea, even if I could set the closest attendee on fire with a flutter of my wings.

Shit… Would giving up my crown to Pietr mean giving up my fiery wings?

A dilemma for another day.

Adam spread his wings wide, his white feathers almost blinding even in the low lighting. He raised his voice to be heard over the din, "If I may?"

Instantly, the arguing and chatter stopped, all inhumanly beautiful faces turning to listen, even Bianca's. Bringing the archangel was definitely a smart idea. I forgot how much pull the DEA had over the global Community, even royalty.

Vincenzo nodded at Adam.

"While the agency cannot directly interfere in the Community's business unless said business impacts the health and wellbeing of others," the archangel said, "we are in agreement that you allow Ms. Neill's participation in the Blood Trials."

Philip, the blond-haired man who spoke up earlier, assessed me from head to foot, his arousal becoming more pronounced beneath his pants. "For what purpose? What's your motive?"

"The dragonstone," I said simply. "It belongs to me."

His chuckle was dark and humorless. "And we should just grant anyone who claims ownership of the gem the right to fight?"

Vincenzo narrowed his eyes, red flashing through his pupils. "Watch yourself, Philip. Your accusation suggests we didn't vet our guest and her claim."

"Forgive me, Your Majesty," Philip said, though sarcasm was evident in his tone. Someone needed a spanking.

Desire spiked between my legs, and the handsome vampire glanced at me with a knowing smirk.

Ugh. Wrong kind of spanking.

Holding his gaze, I burned out his *influence*, smiling as he grimaced.

"The dragons created the stone for one of my ancestors," I explained. "It was stolen from my family, and since you refuse to return it to its rightful owner, I'm willing to fight to get it back."

A rumble of anger moved through the crowd at my not-so-subtle jab.

A woman with long, light brown hair and dark hazel eyes stepped closer, placing a hand on Philip's arm before he could speak. His eyes flashed dangerously, but if she was concerned, she didn't show it.

She also didn't display a hint of embarrassment over her half-naked state in front of strangers. The top of her pale pink dress gathered at her waist, and I had to work seriously hard not to glance at her voluptuous breasts every few seconds.

So much for being glad that Bianca wasn't naked.

"Does she understand the terms of the contract?" the woman asked in a thick French accent.

No, I certainly did not. I glanced at the king and queen, waiting for an explanation.

Bianca's eyes sparkled with excitement. "We thought it best to get the conclave's agreement before outlining the terms. Perhaps that was the wrong approach, Charlotte?"

A shiver ran up my spine. Even Adam furrowed his eyebrows.

The Blood Trials were a highly guarded secret among the vampiric community. Colin had been the one with the most information, and even that was limited. All I knew was the reputation of complete brutality.

Nothing about this contract.

From my studies with Kit, I knew Charlotte Blanchet was the Master Vampiress of Paris. Unlike the majority here tonight, she had earned her title only within the last decade. She'd been alive far longer than that, of course, but she had only just survived the trials, like, yesterday in their eyes. Her fresh memories might have explained her sympathetic gaze.

"Should you lose, at any level of the trials, your life is forfeit," she said.

"I don't plan on dying."

She tilted her head to one side. "I do not doubt that is your intent. However, I do not mean death, considering your ability to resurrect. Instead, you would become one of us. A vampire for all eternity."

My stomach turned to stone, a heavy rock of despair. I didn't have a choice. Gods above, I fucking hated vampires.

Thane sucked in a sharp breath, then immediately fell into a coughing fit. He pulled out his handkerchief, holding it to his mouth.

Charlotte's nostrils flared, flicking her gaze toward him. She drew her eyebrows together. "You are dying, yes?"

A murmur swept through the room.

Telling them the whole truth wasn't on our agenda. I wasn't sure how this crowd would take our situation, but there was only one way to find out.

Except the archangel beat me to the punch.

Adam turned toward us with a smile, opening an arm as if introducing us for the first time. "The gods have seen fit to bind together a phoenix and a grim reaper. A soul bond that defies our understanding and logic and requires the dragonstone to complete.

"Thane has chosen his final death should we fail in our attempt to heal him. Let them fulfill their sacred duty to the gods." He paused, turning his divine gaze on the undead attendees. Their nudity didn't seem to faze him in the slightest. "Help them."

Damn. He said that so much better than I would have. The reaper's warm hand slipped into mine as the vampires started arguing again.

The king held up his hand, silencing the room. He narrowed his eyes at me. "Is it even possible to turn a phoenix? Would she retain her resurrection ability?"

Adam spread his hands. "We do not have those answers. I do not believe we will find out, either."

I smiled at him. Who knew the archangel had such faith in me?

"If you would be so kind as to give us the room," Vincenzo said, "we will discuss the matter."

Adam bowed his head. "Of course."

Lena and Ivan met us at the top of the two staircases and followed us into the muraled hallway. The door closed behind us, silencing the discussion inside. With so many secrets to keep, there must be some fantastic insulation in this building.

Two vampires stood guard, either to keep us from entering or snooping. I was sure there were more bloodsuckers close by, too, hiding in dark corners like the vermin they were.

Waving the others toward the middle of the hall, we formed a small circle.

"How long do you think this will take?" I asked, keeping my voice low.

"You do not need to worry about them overhearing. I have cloaked our conversation," Adam said.

I glanced at the vampires at the doors and raised my voice. "I hope Tweedle Dee and Tweedle Dum over there don't find out we're about to bomb the building."

Not a twitch from either guard.

Lena smacked my arm.

"Ow!" I rubbed at the spot, glaring at her. "You're not supposed to hit your tsarina. What was that for?"

"I can when it's warranted," she muttered. "What if it hadn't worked, you *drochit?*"

"Oh, I trust Adam's ability." I waved a hand dismissively. "I just wanted to have a little fun with it."

"To answer your question regarding time," the archangel cut in as Lena opened her mouth again, "I do not know. As you saw, there was disagreement from some of the others."

"I mean, Bianca wasn't exactly thrilled about the idea

either." I looked at Ivan and Lena. "Did you guys hear anything we can use if they say no?"

Ivan rubbed his chin thoughtfully. "I didn't think so at first, but I keep coming back to it. Do the fae and vampires have any kind of business relationship?"

"Vampires don't exactly get along with any members of the Community outside their own," Thane explained. "They're tolerated at best. What kind of business?"

"I'm not sure," Ivan said, his eyebrows furrowed thoughtfully. "A passing comment about the fae queen and a vampire named Emilia."

The fae queen and a Master Vampiress? That was a weird connection. It was also odd that I had thought about Emilia earlier tonight for the first time in weeks.

"That outspoken one cut the conversation short when he noticed me," Ivan continued.

"Philip?" I asked.

He nodded. "His whole attitude suggested a superiority complex. Total narcissist."

I could definitely see that. The vampire hadn't struck me as a man who liked to follow others.

"Anyway, talk of the fae reminded me I've never been to the Otherworld," Ivan said. "I plan on going after this is all over."

Lena started questioning him about the fae, and the two wandered away to discuss their next great adventure.

"Do you know anything about Queen Fiadh and Lady Emilia working on something together?" Thane asked Adam.

The angel's eyes were narrowed in contemplation. "No. I do not, which is a concerning thought. I will look into it upon our return."

After an hour of waiting around and listening to them discuss boring agency stuff, I needed to sit. My feet were killing me just standing around doing nothing in high heels.

I sat on one of the black velvet wingback chairs, sinking into its cushion, and immediately wanted to fall asleep. Sitting might have been a bad idea.

Thane took the chair next to me while Adam continued to stand in the middle of the hall, his hands clasped serenely in front of him. Patient like only an angel could be.

I held my hand out, and Thane took it. "How're you doing?"

He smirked. "Oh, you know, slowly decaying on the inside. I'm great."

That imagery was rather disgusting. "I walked into that one."

"I'm fine." His thumb stroked the back of my hand. "I'm more worried about you at this point. If they let you fight, but also if they don't."

"Afraid of what crazy idea I'll come up with next?"

He grinned. "Absolutely."

"I guess I have a history of crazy ideas," I said with a slight shrug. "Someone has to keep us on our toes."

"You certainly do that."

We sat in silence for a while, and I did my best to put my anxious thoughts to rest. I must have put them to rest a little too well because one of the guards startled me out of a light doze.

He opened the door. "They're ready for you."

CHAPTER 19

Thursday Evening

We returned to the conclave, and for the second time that evening, all eyes were on us as we descended the stairs. Vincenzo and Bianca met us at the bottom, and the rest of the vampires gathered around. Most had donned some sort of clothing or robe, and the king had closed and tied his.

"The conclave has made a decision," Vincenzo announced.

I held my breath, afraid the slightest movement might change the outcome.

"We will permit you to fight."

Behind me, Lena grumbled, and Thane's grip on my hand tightened. My heart thudded in my chest.

It was happening—for real. I was going to win the stone and save Thane's life.

I dipped my head. "Thank you."

"We'd like to remind you of the cost should you lose during any part of the trials," the king warned. "Once you sign the contract, there is no turning back."

Only vampires would have a contract for a literal blood bath. "Understood."

"The trials begin one week from tonight. We'll have the paperwork drawn up before you leave." He raised his glass and flashed a lecherous grin. "Now, let us enjoy the rest of the evening."

Sultry music drifted from the speakers once again, and the vampires returned to conversations they had abandoned hours ago as if they had never stopped to decide a woman's fate.

And by conversations, I meant sexcapades.

I turned to face my friends, each of their expressions deadly serious.

"Veronica," Thane said, reaching up to stroke my cheek. "I love that you are willing to risk so much to save my life. But it's too much. I can't let you do this."

I leaned into the warmth his touch always provided. "No one *lets* me do anything. I'm a grown-ass woman, and I make my own decisions."

"Well, *this* grown-ass woman agrees with your man," Lena said, hands on her hips. "I didn't actually think they'd agree to it."

"Seriously, why does everyone underestimate me and

my level of desperation?" I asked, not exactly looking for a response.

"While I wish there was another way," Adam said, "I have faith in Ms. Neill's abilities to succeed."

Ivan snagged a glass off the tray of a passing server. "Make that two of us." He sniffed the contents of the glass, grimaced, and replaced the glass. "Blood—not what I was hoping for."

Lena glared at Ivan. "You only agree with the angel to get on her good side."

"Whether or not that's true," I said, "I'm going to need all of your help to prepare. I need to be able to win without my magic."

～w～

After declining several invitations to join in on the fun— which became harder to resist with each passing minute—I followed up on the contract's status with Vincenzo. It had been ready the whole time, of course.

The Blood Trials contract required a blood signature. No big surprise there. After each page was marked with my red thumbprint, Bianca made sure to tell me I couldn't use my magic in the arena. Based on her smug look, she must have thought I didn't know that tidbit before her declaration.

Too bad for her, it was one of the few things I *did* know thanks to Colin.

Adam promised me the DEA's facilities for training and offered up anyone I wanted to work with within the agency. Basically, the agency was at my complete disposal, which felt pretty damn awesome even if it was for a shitty cause. We agreed to meet at an ungodly hour in the morning to begin training.

Just as Ivan's eyes glowed with the impending jump back to Miami, the vampire crowd shifted, and I caught sight of Emilia. I thought it was her, anyway. We were gone too fast to be certain.

The more I thought about it, though, I was pretty sure it wasn't her. From Kit's research, I knew it wasn't normal for other associations to attend foreign conclaves or trials, and vampires were all about traditions and rules. I was sure thinking about her earlier in the evening caused the mistaken identity.

Dawn had arrived in Italy by the time we finally returned to Miami, where it wasn't even midnight yet.

When we got back to the penthouse, I sent Kit a few texts explaining everything that had occurred and our plan going forward. She promised to find out everything she could about the trials that could give me a leg up. I hoped that meant she had forgiven me or was working her way there.

Five hours of fitful sleep later, I entered the DEA's gymnasium, stifling a yawn. I took a sip of the fresh coffee I'd snagged before arriving and looked around. Despite the exhaustion proudly displaying itself as lovely puffy eyelids and filling my limbs with lead, my eyebrows shot up.

The place was huge, like several high school gyms packed into one giant rectangle kind of huge. Three-story climbing walls covered one area to my right, weights and various exercise machines came next, and an elaborate obstacle course complete with pools of water took up the middle.

Several fully enclosed rooms with transparent walls took up a good chunk of the gym's left side. Those would be for magical training, keeping any accidents to a minimum and messes much easier to clean up. Above my head, a track ran around the entire perimeter, allowing runners a chance to watch the activities happening below.

"Wow," I murmured, taking another sip.

I hadn't expected the DEA to provide such delicious coffee. Or maybe it had just been so long since I'd had the real stuff that anything would taste good.

Don't get me wrong, *kofe* in Mirfeniksa was good for getting me going in the mornings, but not nearly as tasty as a fresh human-made brew. Maybe humans had their own kind of magic when it came to coffee.

"The agency does it right," Thane said beside me, pride in his voice as he gazed around.

I glanced at him with a smile. "Miss it already?"

"Oh God, no." He grinned. "Too much of my blood and sweat was spilled in here."

"No tears?" I teased.

"Maybe a few," he admitted.

Lena stepped up on my other side, her mouth hanging open. "Pietr has got to see this."

His mouth too full of a fist-sized chocolate muffin to comment, Ivan simply nodded. His wide eyes spoke volumes.

I took a bigger sip of my steaming coffee, ingesting as much caffeine as I could before I had to put it down. "Where do we start?"

Fortunately—or unfortunately, depending on how I looked at it—my friends did not go easy on me. The next few days were a whirlwind as I trained, ate, and slept like the dead every night. Perfecting my fighting skills with various weapons and without, and learning everything I could about vampire culture.

Through Kit's research—which included some hefty bribes—we discovered a few more details about the four fights, each one harder than the last, like Colin had said. Each contest had a purpose, even if it was just for the observers' sadistic enjoyment.

The first would be for the newly-turned, who were usually caught up in blood lust. A handful of several hundred-year-old vampires joined in, trying to advance to the Elite Guard, in which they would protect Masters and royalty. The fight continued for a set time and whoever was still alive at the end moved on to the next trial.

The second battle would be members of the Elite Guard seeking promotion to Master of a city. While it wasn't technically the most challenging fight, only one would be left standing. Because the chances of survival were so slim, only a few guards competed in each quarterly trial.

The cream of the crop, if you will.

Or, since they loved gardening so much, the best carrots of the bunch.

In between fighting sessions, Kit had me memorizing the names and faces of the European vampire elite. The sessions with her were also a crash course in the workings of upper-class vampire society. Despite my general distaste for bloodsuckers and studying, I found it all quite intriguing.

Ivan and Thane joined us from time to time, chiming in or asking questions about a particular vampire.

During physical training in the afternoons, everyone

jumped in to provide a multi-attack approach like I would see in the first two fights. No matter how much money we threw at the few vampires willing to talk, we couldn't find out much about the last two fights.

So, each of my friends also took turns trying to take me down one-on-one. They all fought differently, and Ivan was incredibly sneaky. He thrived on fighting dirty.

Lena was a relentless machine, finding new weaknesses and unguarded spots on my person just when I was getting confident that I would take her down. I'd become complacent in my new position as tsarina, letting the day-to-day activities take priority.

Not anymore. Once I got that dragonstone, I'd focus on keeping my mind and body in fighting shape.

As much as Thane wanted to continue sparring, he had to stop early by the third day. Panting heavily, he wiped the sweat off his forehead with a towel. His usually tan face looked ashen, and his hands shook.

I stood in front of him and put my hands on his chest. His slick skin was cooler to the touch than normal. "You need to rest."

"I can rest when I'm dead," he growled, anger emanating from his entire being. I knew it wasn't directed at me.

"Hundreds of years from now, yes." I reached up and pulled his face to mine, brushing my lips against his. There was still some warmth in him, but it was fading quickly. "Don't rush into it. Please."

His shoulders sagged, and he wrapped his arms around my waist. Our foreheads touched as he sighed. His blue gaze met mine. "I'm not good at sitting on the sidelines."

I rubbed my nose against his. "I know, and I definitely like watching you move. But you're just as good at research. Why don't you help Kit for a while? Regain some strength before joining in again?"

His thumbs rubbed my hips in an absentminded gesture. "I don't think the dying process works that way."

I knew that as well as he did, but I'd be damned if I was going to give up hope.

Hope might be the only thing keeping me going right now.

The next day, I sat with Kit and massaged a kink in my shoulder. I didn't know why I even bothered—everything hurt.

We were in one of the DEA's conference rooms that Adam had booked solely for our use. Kit had taken up residence over the past few days, which meant she'd set up two laptops and three monitors on the table.

Papers, folders, and empty takeout containers spread across the remaining surface as she followed every possible lead about the Blood Trials. She had an impressive number of secret sources willing to give her most of the information we wanted.

For a price, of course.

Angela came and went, bringing food and coffee to her fiancée. Although she always had a smile on her face, there was an obvious distance between them, both emotionally and physically. I knew it was because of the visit Kit would need to pay Octavia, a fact she hadn't shared with Angela yet.

"Does shifting count as using my magic?" I asked.

"No, shifting's just part of your genetics," Kit answered without pausing her typing. "Don't ask me to explain the difference, but not allowing you to shift would be like not allowing them to use their fangs. Trust me, they will do their very best to shred you to pieces with those suckers."

I smiled as she focused on her work, totally unaware of the pun she'd just made. Typical Kit, and I loved it.

After learning that fantastic detail, Ivan taught me a new trick back in the gym—a partial shift. Doing so allowed me to grow razor-sharp falcon talons from my fingers while leaving the rest of me intact. The feeling took some getting used to, and honestly, it wasn't a pretty sight.

With any luck, the weirdness would throw the vampires off a bit and give me an advantage. At the very least, it would be leveling the playing field against their claws.

And I would need all the help I could get.

CHAPTER 20

Wednesday Afternoon

The day before we left for war was a frenzy of activity as everyone prepared. Warriors assessed their armor and weapons for any weaknesses, healers gathered supplies, and those staying behind ensured they had everything they'd need to survive if no one returned. It was a grim thought, but a necessary one. Despite all that, an excited chatter echoed throughout every hall and cavern.

The day before the first trial was set to begin, I felt pretty damn confident about my chances of winning. My body was stronger than ever before, and my muscle memory was honed and ready for just about anything.

Unfortunately, I was also nervous as hell and beyond worried about Thane's worsening condition. His skin had taken on a greenish hue, and bloody noses were a daily nuisance. Sometimes several in one day.

The good news was his attitude. He had kept his head held high and thrown himself into research. His confidence in me was such a huge turn-on.

Sadly, we wouldn't be getting down and dirty again until I won that stone.

Carrying a takeout bag from a nearby Chinese place, I walked down the nearly empty corridor toward Thane's office. He still didn't need calories, but I certainly did. Catching a whiff of the tangy sauce, my stomach grumbled audibly, angry that I'd chosen to wait until after the lunch rush.

Too bad, stomach.

I was so over answering the incessant questions from other grim reapers and even a handful of angels. Not that they ate lunch, but they came out in droves at the predictable hour knowing that I did. Everyone wanted to hear about how training was progressing and anything I learned about the Blood Trials. I didn't want to be rude, but the questions never ceased.

To avoid that today, I'd chosen a less busy route to Thane's office, using a back stairwell rather than walk past the open cubicle area. Only closed doors, a few printers collecting dust, and potted plants watched me pass.

Ivan jogged up to my side, an envelope in hand. "This came for you today."

Raising an eyebrow, I glanced at the handwriting. I didn't recognize it. "Can you open it for me?"

He sliced open the flap and removed the letter just as we arrived at the door to Thane's office. Hooking the plastic bag over my arm, I reached for the door handle.

Ivan's hand stopped me.

"Read this first." He took the bag from me and handed me the paper, an unfamiliar expression on his face. Kind of grim.

Giving him a curious glance, I did as told:

Dearest Veronica,

Not everything is as it seems. The true threat remains hidden. Waiting. Angry.

Open your eyes, little bird. Dig deeper. I'll see you soon.

Yours Truly,

A Loyal Friend

My blood chilled within me, and the words blurred together. What I was thinking was impossible.

I had seen Xavier's skull mounted in the Miami vampires' nest. Lady Emilia, Miami's newest head vampire, had freely admitted killing him as an example to the others.

The Master Vampire who'd wanted to enslave me was dead. For real dead. He had to be. Plus, he wasn't the only one to call me little bird. Emilia and William had also used the term. Any number of people could have written this letter.

Except Xavier was the only one who'd warned me about a true threat, about William. At least that's who I thought he had meant once the Society of the Dead had come back to life in full force. We'd handled that problem, sweeping the necromancers and their little society back under the rug of obscurity and into prison.

What other threat could still be out there?

I met Ivan's worried gaze and crumpled up the letter with shaking hands. "I don't want Thane to see this."

The last thing my reaper needed was another thing to worry about.

"I had the same thought." He took the letter from me before I could throw it away, tucking it into one of his pockets instead. Refusing to give me back the food, he nodded his head toward the office. "Just in case you shake too much."

I gave him a thankful smile and opened the door. Blood splattered across Thane's desk and onto the chairs in front of it. Two legs stuck out from behind the desk.

"Thane!" I ran toward the desk.

Ivan yelled for help down the hallway.

The reaper who'd stolen my heart and soul lay crumpled on the ground, foaming blood oozing from his mouth and nose. I fell to my knees beside him and felt for a pulse. The beat was faint, but his skin was clammy and cold.

Hands pulled me out of the way, and angels took my place by Thane's side.

"No! I need to stay with him," I pleaded, the room already blurry with tears.

"Veronica," a familiar voice called my name—Jessa, my guardian angel, the one with the most gorgeous lagoon-colored eyes.

I collapsed into her outstretched arms, sobs wracking my body. She soothed my hair and led me out of the office. Two angels carried Thane out on a stiff board and headed down the corridor.

"Where are they taking him?" I asked, trying to pull away from her to follow.

"Give them some space, Veronica," she said, holding me back a few feet. "He'll be okay. They're taking him to the hospital wing, and we'll go, too. Just don't crowd them."

I let her lead me behind them, feeling like my whole world was about to crumble. Like my heart was about to shatter into a million pieces, too many to ever put back together again.

What kind of cruel gods did we have to let this happen? Was their goal just to take away everyone I loved? What had I done to deserve this?

Would Kit be next?

I clenched my teeth and wiped my face with my hand. Like fuck I'd let them take Thane *or* Kit from me. Adam told us this would be a slow and painful process, and I had to believe that Thane would hold on. No matter what my eyes wanted to make me think, I knew he wasn't gone yet.

I still had time.

Hours later, I sat beside Thane's hospital bed, running my fingers up and down his forearm. I had pulled the blue blanket up and tucked it around his waist. A white hospital gown covered his chest and shoulders.

He hadn't woken yet, a fact that scared the bejeezus out of me, but Jessa reassured me that this was completely normal.

I had to trust her.

Not only was she my friend, but she was also one of the resident healing angels. She'd patched me up more than once. Unfortunately, there was only so much the angels could do for a dying reaper who'd chosen this path. Interfering with their god's plan for a soul wasn't possible.

The machines hooked up to him, monitoring his vitals, continued to beep at steady intervals, confirmation that his heart continued to beat. He still held on.

"You know, I still haven't asked you what you were before you died," I said, barely above a whisper. "What type of Community member you were."

I leaned forward and rested my arms on the bed, my chin on my arms. I watched his chest rise and fall with his breaths. For a dead guy, he sure looked alive. Smiling sadly, I remembered how I'd tried to resist the temptation in the beginning. How I thought it'd be too gross being with a dead guy.

How wrong I had been.

I had fallen hard, and he had proven to be so full of life, so vibrant. I longed to spend the rest of my life with him.

"I still have so much to learn about you," I whispered, my voice cracking. "You can't leave me before I get to ask you all my questions, and it's a long list. So, don't even think about giving up on me, okay?"

The door creaked open behind me, but I didn't bother to turn and look. I was too tired. Soft footsteps came close, and a gentle hand touched my shoulder.

"He's going to be okay," Kit's calm voice said. "This is just a bump in the road."

I reached up and rested my hand on hers, appreciating the comfort. "I know, but how am I supposed to leave him like this tomorrow?"

"Jessa is confident he'll wake up by tomorrow morning," she said.

"What if he pushed himself too hard, and his body doesn't have anything left to give?"

"Veronica, look at me." Her voice was kind but firm with the mom tone she used without realizing it.

I unfolded my arms from the bed and turned to face her. She sat in the chair next to mine and took my hands, a surprising gesture coming from her. She meant business.

"What happens to Thane at this point is out of your control," she said, her gaze searing into mine. "What *is* in your control is tomorrow. The first of the Blood Trials. Focus on that. Channel your rage and grief and fear into every ounce of your being and tear those bloodsucking motherfuckers limb from limb."

I raised my eyebrows at her vicious words.

"Destroy every last one of them," she continued, "the so-called best of their best. Show them what a terrible mistake they made by not returning an item stolen from you. Show them what they've given up by becoming the undead creatures that they are, the *life* that separates us from them."

Goosebumps rose along my arms. Damn. She was really good at this whole hyping someone up before the battle thing. I really wished she could come with me.

"I'm coming with you," she said as if reading my thoughts.

"Not happening. If Thane…" I bit off my words, not willing to say them out loud. "I need you alive."

She let my hands go, likely reaching her limit for physical touch. "Angela is helping me with a spell that will hide my identity. They'll have no idea."

I blinked. "Angela agreed to this?"

"It was her idea." A smile tugged at her lips. "She knows you're like a little sister to me. I wouldn't be able to forgive myself if I wasn't by your side."

I wiped a stray tear from my cheek. "Godsdamnit, Kit. I didn't want to cry again."

She stood. "You can stay for another hour, but then Ivan is coming to take your place." She raised a hand as I opened my mouth. "It's not up for debate. You want to help Thane? Then get some rest and kick ass tomorrow."

Her gaze moved to Thane for a brief moment, softening.

After she left, I returned my arms to the bed and leaned my chin on them again. I knew she and my friends were right. The best thing I could do for Thane right now was fight. And he better fucking hold on until I returned.

Because if he died while I fought for my life, for *his* life, then everything would have been for nothing. There was no way my heart would survive that.

The only silver lining?

Neither would the vampires.

CHAPTER 21

Thursday Night

My heart thudded hard against my ribs, turning my pulse into a roaring monster inside my eardrums. As Lena tightened my armor's straps and checked for any noticeable gaps, I glanced down the dark hallway.

Just outside the closed doors, beneath the moon's pale light, the trials were set to begin.

The ancient coliseum—not *the* Colosseum, but a near-replica created in the Italian countryside by one of the previous vampire kings—would house the fights over the next four nights. The king had turned the architect into a vampire just to finish the project. It was designed specifically for the original Blood Trials, back before there were global divisions.

Above our heads, dust drifted down from the ceiling, and a thunderous din spoke to the sheer volume of vampires in attendance.

To watch a fucking bloodbath.

That's all this was. A glorified slaughter. Especially now that I'd arrived.

I clenched and unclenched my fists.

Jessa had been wrong—Thane didn't wake up that morning or that afternoon. I was forced to leave his side, but she had promised to call as soon as he woke up. Our phones had been confiscated as a precaution to keep the trials a mystery, but Vincenzo assured me I'd be notified immediately.

The promise helped—

No, actually, it didn't.

If it wasn't for the stupid trial rules, I would go home after every fight to be by Thane's side and only come back to prepare for the next one. Not so much. The rules stated that the contestants and their assistants must remain on the premises in the holding rooms provided.

No exceptions.

I was crushed that I wouldn't be able to see those ocean blue eyes that saw straight down into my soul one more time before the fight. I was terrified I never would again.

In the hour since we'd arrived at the coliseum, an emissary had gone over basic details and led our party to our holding area, where we prepared and waited.

Armor and physical weapons of any kind were permitted; poisons, potions, and weaponized magic were strictly forbidden. Three gong strikes would indicate it was time for fighters to take our places. A single gong shortly after meant the doors would open, and the trial would begin.

Whether I stepped through the doors or not, there was no turning back—my red thumbprint stained the contract. If I lost, I would be enslaved for the next few centuries until I followed my parents' footsteps and returned to the sun.

There was no rushing that process, either. Dazhbog would only allow the ceremony when it was time. I prayed that he would show me mercy.

Of course, returning to the sun would only happen if they failed to turn me into a vampire. If they succeeded, there was no telling what would become of me.

Dark red smears marked the stone walls everywhere we looked, and a distinct metallic scent was prevalent. The vampire with us didn't seem to think it was a problem that the place hadn't been cleaned since the last trials. I supposed they considered it would just be a waste of time. That or it acted as a fighting aphrodisiac for them.

Ivan popped into my vision as he buckled on my sword belt. "Don't forget what I taught you."

I nodded. My talons would make for a special surprise—special and bloody.

Continuing to tuck knives into various hidden sheaths stitched into my leather armor, he added, "Don't forget what Pietr taught you, either."

I pulled my eyebrows together in confusion before I caught his meaning. His gaze darted toward the vampire attending us.

During our first spar, Pietr had asked me why I wasn't turning my flame inward, on myself. Using magic that way wasn't technically against the rules; only weaponized magic was. They didn't need to know I could use my inner fire to boost myself to goddess-like levels.

Oh, this was going to be fun.

The gong's deep boom reverberated across the coliseum, sounding three times. A deafening roar surged from the crowd. It was such a shame I couldn't turn myself into a bomb and just be done with it all like I had with the Risen.

Sadly, that would pit the rest of the vampiric world against me, and I really didn't want to have to deal with that mess. Adam wouldn't be too pleased either.

A sharp pain lanced through my heart as I remembered the stadium. That was the day Thane had learned what I really was when I resurrected from the dust after destroying the zombie army. He had kissed me right before I went nuclear, slowing time with some rare reaper ability.

I better get another kiss like that from him soon.

"Your Majesty, it's time to take your place," the vampire attendant said with a bow and gestured down the dark hall leading up and out.

Angela stepped in front of me. Except, it wasn't actually Angela—this was Kit's disguise.

The ruse was genius. If any vampires looked into her background, they would see she was human and already part of our circle. As an added precaution for any snoopers back in Miami, Adam had invited the real Angela to stay at the DEA building for the next few nights.

She reached up and put her delicate, uncalloused hands on my shoulders. Such a difference between the two women. "You got this, V. This is the easy one. Don't reveal all your cards yet, and don't try to be a fucking hero."

I took a deep breath and nodded. She was right—I needed to keep some surprises for the last. After a quick squeeze before she could escape, I turned to Ivan and Lena and gave them both tight hugs.

"This isn't goodbye, you *drochit*," Lena muttered as she pulled away.

"No, it's a thank you," I said, smiling. "For being by my side and helping me through this."

Ivan leaned his arm on Lena's shoulder. "And for not telling Pietr, right?"

"Absolutely. If I survive this, he's definitely going to kill me." I winked and turned toward the hall.

No more waiting.

I strode forward until I reached the wooden doors. Through the cracks, sand covered the coliseum floor. I clenched my fists. Some would try to use it against me, and I would be ready.

The deep, soul-rattling boom of the gong sounded again, and the doors swung open.

I stepped into the arena.

Sand scraped beneath my boots. A cool breeze brushed past my face, bringing with it the salty scent of the nearby sea. Encircling the entire arena, torches' orange-red flames danced in the wind, casting moving shadows in every direction.

Raising my gaze, rows upon rows of vampires filled the stadium benches. The unobscured moon's light washed their faces with an eerie paleness. They cheered and laughed above my head, circling all around. Thousands of them surrounded me.

My skin crawled, and my fingers twitched. Instinct itched to send a fireball straight into that soulless crowd.

Unlike the rest of the Community, vampires had no souls. They traded them in for everlasting life on earth. When they died the second time, their bodies returned to their previous forms, which in most cases was dust and dry bones.

Then they just ceased to exist.

On the first level to my right was a covered podium with two thrones and several other fancy chairs—the royalty box. Or Imperial box, if they went by Roman terminology. Vincenzo and Bianca sat on their thrones, watching and waiting.

Through five other open doors, three men and two women strode onto the sand. These were the older vampires who sought a place among the Elite Guard. They embodied inhuman beauty and grace despite their hardened expressions, and they gripped their weapons loosely as if there was nothing to fear.

That was their first mistake, and also their last.

The final six doors opened. Streaming forth, the newly-turned bent their gangly limbs awkwardly as they tried to push past each other. Their laughter filled the arena like the high-pitched cackle of a hyena approaching its prey. Excitement rippled through the onlookers as the new ones kept coming, dozens of them rushing forward to find something to kill.

To eat.

The older vamps leaped into action, sending limbs and heads rolling with deadly accuracy. Sensing the immediate threat, the wave of newly-turned surrounded the five older ones. Their laughter became ravenous snarls and growls.

The first time I'd faced six vampires, I'd felt outnumbered. I was a good fighter, well trained by my father, but half a brood was a lot for me then. Especially knowing there were six more watching us from above, waiting to take the fallen one's places.

I drew one of my new wooden knives and slid the blade across my palm. Blood splattered the sand beneath my hand before the wound sealed itself shut.

The effect was immediate.

Every vampire on the ground and even some above snapped their gazes toward me. White fangs flashed in the moonlight. The tide turned, and dozens of vampires headed straight for me, including those hoping to join the Elite.

My phoenix blood was too potent to resist.

I smiled.

Still holding the knife in one hand, I drew Lisa and gave her a twirl to loosen my wrist.

The first few who had been the fastest reached me. I sliced through the closest one's neck, decapitating it. My blade was sharp, but these newer vamps also lacked solid muscle, sending them back to the grave easier.

Blood spurted from its neck, and the reanimation magic fled from the creature. The body and head dropped to the sand at my feet, turning to dust and brittle bones.

I whirled to chop down the next, swinging my knife up to stab another through the heart. The wooden blade did its job well.

Moving through them like a surging wave, a tsunami intent on mass destruction, I took two then three down in quick, successive strokes. Stab through the skull, slice through the neck, pierce the heart. Blood splashed in all directions. Nothing but dust and bone left in my wake again and again.

The wannabe Elites caught up to the swarm and fought their way through to me. Judging by the hunger glinting in their undead eyes, they still thought they were going to take me down.

They had no idea who they were dealing with.

I wasn't the unseasoned girl in the alley from before. The cocky girl who thought taking down six new vampires would be tough, but not impossible.

No, I'd become so much more. I'd faced a Master Vampire and lived—twice—ended the life of the fae necromancer responsible for bringing down reapers and angels, and destroyed the woman who took my family from me.

Now, I was a warrior. I was a queen, and the man I loved more than life itself stood on death's precipice. I would stop at *nothing* to bring him back from the edge, safe and whole.

I ducked beneath a blade. The sting of its kiss bit into my arm. Clenching my teeth, I dipped to the side and came back swinging. I lunged through a cloud of dust, impaling the next vampire on Lisa. I followed up with a thrust through his skull.

The last few vampires lowered their weapons and stepped back, panting and seething. Their eyes burned with hatred and unsatisfied craving.

It took me a moment to realize the gong had sounded. The first trial had ended, and only four of us remained.

I'd survived.

CHAPTER 22

Thursday Night

“I said *don't* be a fucking hero!” Glaring at me, Kit—wearing Angela's skin—smacked me upside the head.

“Ow!” I flinched away, expecting another hit. “I wasn't being a hero. I was just getting the job done faster. Why is smacking me your new thing?”

She shook her dainty white finger at me. “You know perfectly well that's not all you did out there. Now they're going to be gunning for you.”

I let out an exasperated huff, ignoring Lena's matching glare as she helped me out of my sweaty armor. She and Ivan refused to let me help clean my armor or weapons, even though I caught her grimace when her nose got too close to an overly bloody piece.

"They were always going to be gunning for me," I said.

Since the holding room would also serve as our bedroom after each trial, four cots had been pushed against the walls while I'd been fighting. Lena carried my armor to some hooks on an opposite wall and started cleaning it.

"She's got a point," Ivan said from his perch. He half-sat on a stool, one foot still on the ground, while he cleaned my weapons.

"Stop being such a kiss-ass," Lena snapped, turning to flick blood from her hand in his direction.

The newer vamps didn't bleed much, but the wannabe Elites sure did before their bodies rapidly decayed. Why their undead hearts even continued to beat was a mystery. Maybe to fit in better with the human population, making it easier to sneak up on unsuspecting prey.

He raised his arm and ducked, but the drops didn't make it that far. "I'm not kissing her ass. Didn't you hear the crowd's cheers change? They wanted Veronica to win."

I frowned. I hadn't heard the yelling at all once the fight began. Talk about focus.

"How the hell does that help us?" Kit asked, brushing Angela's unruly brown curls away from her face in annoyance. Her usual look was half a shaved head and braids for a reason—she hated hair.

"Knowing that their kind is rooting for an outsider will make them angry," he explained. "They'll let their emotions affect their decisions."

I bent to grab a cloth from the water bucket and squeezed the excess from the fabric. "You assume vampires have emotions."

I wiped blood and dirt from my face. Not dirt—dust. As in ground vampire guts. I crinkled my nose. Gross.

"They might be buried deep, but they're in there," he said, focused on the blade in his hand. He turned it over, checking his work.

"Actually, you're right," I said, dipping the cloth into the bucket to rinse it.

"Why do you sound surprised?" He looked up at me, crestfallen.

I laughed and ran the cloth over my arms. "Not at you. I'm surprised I forgot. Xavier was easier to manipulate when I taunted him about his toxic masculinity."

Mentioning Xavier reminded me of the letter I'd received in the DEA office. I forgot all about it once I found Thane unconscious. Looking into who sent the note would give us something to do between fights.

Kit-Angela paced the length of the room. She snapped her fingers and stopped, her eyes brightening in a way only Angela's could. "Okay, then we use that excitement to your advantage. They're seeing something that's never happened before. Or hasn't for a really long time—an outsider. Show them something new tomorrow. Make them go wild."

I mean, she didn't have to tell me twice.

⩗

The second trial was going to be interesting. And by interesting, I meant tough—for most people, anyway.

Along with fighting, my parents had also taught me the importance of positive self-talk.

199

Think confident, be confident.

Except, I didn't need that lesson today.

Jessa had called. Thane still hadn't woken up. Terror gripped every part of me in a vice and wouldn't let go. Not only terror, but also anger. Fury.

Blinding *rage*.

Had the vampires given me back the damn stone, an ancestral item stolen from me, we wouldn't be going through any of this. Now, they were going to pay. They would face the consequences of their selfish actions. Hatred for their kind threatened to consume me.

Clenching my fists, I stepped onto the dark sand. A boom of thunder rolled overhead, and cool raindrops beat against my skin. The torches' fire danced wildly in the storm's wind, which swirled and flung sand with each gust.

I flipped on my ability to see heat signatures and waited.

Six other doors opened, and the Elite Guard stepped out. Because their hearts continued to pump blood through their system, vampires maintained a low level of heat. They glowed bluish-green except where their heart was.

That was a deep red bullseye.

These vicious vampires would fight to become the next Master, but only one of us would remain standing. Six sets of eyes fixated on me.

They must have thought taking me out first would be the best option.

Okay then, fuckers, let's play.

I raised my empty hands and partially shifted, allowing my fingers to warp into wickedly sharp talons. Those closest to me in the crowd and able to see the change whooped and cheered, and the word spread rapidly.

With a cruel smile on my face, I flipped the Elites off.

Snarls and growls accompanied them as they raced toward me, sand flying behind their heels.

This time, I didn't wait for them to come all the way to me.

I sprinted toward the farthest on the right. The sand wasn't soaked yet, so I slid on one leg just as I reached him. His sword's blade swept over my head. I raked at his Achilles tendons, shredding them with my talons. He fell to his knees, screaming.

Back on my feet, I dashed toward the next. I caught his swing on my left vambrace, gritting my teeth as the hit thrummed painfully through my forearm. His blade didn't cut through my armor.

I swiped through his throat with my talons. His eyes widened, and he clutched at the gushing wound. Before he could heal, I pulled a stake from my belt and stabbed it through the pulsing red glow—his heart.

As the vamp's body lost reanimation magic and dissolved, I turned and flung the same stake at the first vampire who was just rising. His ankle wounds had healed. The wood pierced his chest and poked through the other side. With his mouth and chest gaping open, he fell to his knees once again and crumbled into dust.

Two down, four to go.

The raindrops became a steady downpour, and the others closed in, circling me warily. The hatred in their eyes was almost tangible in its intensity. I had proven to be a formidable opponent. More brutal than they expected.

The crowd's chanting grew louder, vibrating against my bones. As I realized they were chanting *my* name, I grinned.

No wonder these Elite vamps were so pissed.

Apparently, Ivan had been right. They did have some emotions, and I loved using them to my advantage.

All four rushed me at the same time.

I blocked a swing and turned to strike another. Sand hit my face. My eyes stung from the contact, and my tongue grated against the roof of my mouth like sandpaper.

Blinking rapidly to clear my vision, I gagged and spat. A sharp object knocked hard against my forehead, sending me into a dizzying stumble.

Something warm and thick dripped into my eye and further obscured my vision—my blood. Before I had a chance to wipe it off or move away, strong hands grabbed my arms. Sharp claws dug into my skin down to my bones, drawing more blood.

Shit.

A stab of fear coursed through me as they gripped tight. I had known some of them would use the sand against me, and I'd still let it happen way too easily. My pulse pounded in my ears, and my eyes burned.

They held my arms out, away from my body, allowing another one a clear shot. Anger sparked back to life, overcoming my fear.

As the blurry figure charged in, I kicked, hoping my aim would knock her blade to the side. I used my momentum to wrench one arm free, snagged another wooden knife from my belt, and staked the one still holding me through the heart.

I shifted into falcon form, tore through the dust cloud, and raked at the remaining three as I passed over their heads. Changing forms cleared my vision enough to continue. As much as I wanted to relish in the freedom of flight, I needed to end this fight.

I tucked my wings into my sides and dove back toward the earth. Screeching my fury, I aimed my talons at one who raised his arms to block me. Skin shredded beneath me.

Aiming for the sand, I shifted back to human form before I landed. My feet touched down, and I whirled in a circle with Lisa. A vampire's head rolled off stiff shoulders and turned to dust before it hit the ground.

When the last vampire fell to her knees, she grasped my wooden stake protruding from her chest. Her body shuddered and disintegrated. A gust of wind swept her away as if she'd never existed.

Panting, I faced the king and queen.

Rain and blood dripped down my arm and off Lisa's blade, soaking into the sand. My wounds would heal in a matter of minutes.

Movement beside Bianca caught my eye.

There was no mistaking the woman this time.

The Master Vampiress of Miami, Emilia Delacroix, sat beside the queen, a smile gracing her full red lips. Her dark brown hair had been pulled up in some sort of fancy bun behind her head and held with two jeweled hair sticks.

I was breaking all kinds of conventions by being here, so it wouldn't have surprised me if the king had extended her an invitation. Since I lived in Miami, I was from—and maybe even representing—her territory. She probably *was* at the conclave, like I thought.

"Congratulations, Your Majesty," Vincenzo called out, his voice carrying in the wind. A sinister look crept over his features. "You've won the title of Master Vampiress. Should you lose either of the next two trials, we'll be delighted to appoint you a city to oversee."

"I'm happy to offer my services training her," Emilia said in her husky yet sultry sex phone operator voice that probably took centuries to master. Or lucky genetics. Her gaze appraised me. "Very happy."

Like a light switch flicking on, her *influence* warmed my body to nearly orgasmic levels. I sucked in a sharp breath, hissing softly as my center pulsed with sudden need. Reaching for my inner flame to burn her out, I found myself resisting…

Myself.

My eyelids fluttered shut. Featherlight touches roamed across my body, caressing my most intimate places. The tiniest moan escaped my lips. My core ached, wanting and needing a release, never wanting her to stop. I craved her fingers inside me, her tongue sucking and flicking against my clit, begging for more until I screamed her name.

The need built. I was about to have a fucking orgasm in front of thousands of people. No, not people—vampires. They would smell my body's betrayal and take turns ravaging me.

And I wanted it to happen.

Just as quickly as it had arrived, the need was gone.

My legs turned to jelly and almost buckled beneath me. I opened my eyes and met her knowing, possessive gaze.

She opened her mouth slightly and ran her tongue along her lips, flicking her fangs. One last pulse of desire swept through me.

Holy fucking shit, she was *strong*. Way stronger than Xavier had been.

"...for your generous offer, Lady Emilia," Vincenzo continued whatever he'd been saying with a sarcastic drawl. He returned his attention to me, apparently unaware of what had just occurred. "We'll take it into consideration when the time comes. The second trial is adjourned."

When. The presumptuous wording snapped the fading threads of her *influence.*

Fear, followed closely by a new wave of fury, replaced any lasting cravings. I didn't know what the fuck Emilia was doing here or what kind of obnoxious game she was playing, but I didn't have time for her shit.

For now, I would keep what happened between us. If I let my friends know what she had done, they would go after her. I couldn't risk anything interfering with the last two trials.

Parched and confused, I turned back to the holding room doors.

Yes, I had survived the second trial, but just barely. I needed to step up my game in the next fight to ensure there would be a fourth. Confidence would only get me so far. The rest was up to my training and my desire, my desperate *need,* to save Thane.

In good news, if I lost, I would earn a new title.

Bad news?

Emilia's *influence* would be too strong to resist.

CHAPTER 23

Friday Night

I needed a shower so fucking bad. This whole using a bucket and a ratty cloth idea was doing absolutely nothing to get the stench of old blood and vampire leftovers out of my pores and definitely not out of my hair. I didn't even want to know what that rat's nest looked like. Not having a mirror had never been so welcome.

"V, you've got a phone call," Kit said behind me.

I turned, my heart leaping into my throat as soon as I saw her smile. Well, Angela's smile. I snatched the phone out of her hands so fast I almost dropped it and pressed the cell to my ear. "Thane?"

"Hey, you." His voice was hoarse and much too quiet. He was still struggling. "I hear you're winning."

Letting out a half-laugh, half-sob, I pressed a hand to my mouth. "You know it. Just kicking ass and taking names. I'm so glad to hear your voice."

I didn't regret my decision to be here, especially now that I was halfway to victory. But I missed him with every godsdamn fiber of my being.

"Two more?" he asked.

"Yeah, the two we haven't learned much about." I immediately wanted to smack myself. I didn't want him to worry. "But the last two were a piece of cake, a walk in the park. Just not the kind with random Risen walking by." I was rambling. "So I'll be back with the stone before you know it."

"V…" A racking cough overtook his words.

Gripping the phone, I felt helpless, completely vulnerable as I listened to his body dying on the other end. How was it fair that I had not only fallen in love with a reaper, but then I had to spend what might be his last days on Earth away from him?

With fucking vampires, no less.

He cleared his throat. "Whatever happens, don't forget that I love you."

"I love you, too." The sting of tears gathered in my eyes. "Don't you dare give up on me."

"Never." His voice faded.

Adam came on the line, "He needs to rest now, Ms. Neill. I promise we will do everything we can."

"Thanks, Adam." I swallowed a hard lump as he ended the call.

I turned to face my friends, my heart about to shatter.

Ivan threw his arm around my shoulders and pulled me to him, hugging me. A moment later, Lena wrapped her arms around us both. And to all of our surprise, Kit-Angela did, too. We stayed like that for a while, drawing comfort and strength from one another.

At least I wasn't facing this alone.

The night of the third trial finally arrived. We spent most of the day doing a whole lot of nothing besides training in our room and trying to figure out who sent the letter using just our collective brainpower. It was becoming more apparent to me that Emilia must have sent the letter.

Xavier was dead, end of story. But I would hardly call her a *loyal friend* after the shit she pulled in the arena the day before.

Because I couldn't tell the others about her yet, our ideas quickly fizzled out. We'd asked more than once if we could wander the halls of the coliseum to get a change of scenery if nothing else, but that was strictly forbidden.

So many rules. The primary reasoning made sense—ensuring no one received aid illegally and maintaining their secretive reputation—but that didn't mean I had to like it. And I certainly wouldn't stop complaining about it in front of the vampire attendant.

If I had to suffer, then so did he.

I pulled vambraces over my forearms, ensuring the fit was as snug as it could be without cutting off circulation. Ivan had done his best to clean them from the night before, but a sticky residue continued to be a nuisance. I was pretty sure it would be best just to burn the whole set once this was over.

The third trial was set to begin any minute now, and we still had no idea what I'd be facing. That it was a fan favorite was the only tidbit Kit had discovered.

Oh goody.

"Whatever you face tonight, you'll knock 'em dead," Lena said, grinning at her own joke.

Behind her back, Ivan rolled his eyes so hard I thought he might hurt himself. I couldn't help but smile. Having these two here with me, lightening the mood, was a godsend.

The gong's three booms shook the room and sprinkled dirt on our heads. After giving my friends a quick hug, I stood at the doors leading into the arena, knife in hand.

Two more to go, and I would be done. I could do this.

I was a fucking queen, for flame's sake.

A single gong sounded, and the doors swung open. The crowd's cheers swept over me. I didn't mind the rain the night before, but I was relieved to find dry sand as I stepped into the moonlight. So much less messy.

Sand absorbed all the bodily fluids flying around during the fights—blood, sweat, tears, and I was sure pee, too—making it easier to clean up. Add rain to the mix, and we're talking a muddy blood bath. Literally.

People stepped out of the eleven other doors, one from each opening. I frowned as my gaze moved from person to person.

What the actual fuck?

These weren't vampires—they were humans and other Community members.

Most people couldn't tell the difference right away, but I had an uncanny ability to sense the *otherness* about supernatural beings. I suddenly remembered Colin's warning, one I'd disregarded then completely forgotten.

Vincenzo stood from his seat, and the crowd quieted. "You will fight until the gong sounds again. Those still alive will receive the gift of immortality, as you've requested." His gaze flicked to me. "Most of you."

Whoa, whoa, whoa. I had agreed to fight vampires, not people wanting to become vampires. That was a huge difference. Colin's warning hadn't really clicked until right now.

Emilia's smile grew with my obvious disgust, and she leaned closer to Bianca. Her lips barely moved, but both women smiled cruelly as their gazes fixated on me.

A flush rose up my neck, and I gripped my knife tighter. I hated what Emilia had done to me, turning my body against me that way. If she was sharing her game with the queen, I was going to have more than just words with Emilia—I'd cut out her heart.

Vincenzo's voice cracked out like a whip, "Begin."

The others didn't waste any time. They rushed toward each other, and steel clashed together like thunder. A whistle whooshed past my ear, followed by a thunk. I turned to find a quivering arrow sticking out of the wooden door.

Fuck!

I had zero interest in killing these idiots who thought vampirism was the best way to live, even if they were going to die anyway to become one. But if I didn't move, I'd face my own death and subsequent bloodsucking life. It didn't matter that I could resurrect—one death and I'd be finished.

The first one reached me—an overly muscled human. Raising his brass-knuckled fists, he grinned, obviously unaware of who he was facing. He probably thought I was an easy target.

I smiled back, and his grin faltered.

That's right, buddy. No damsel in distress here.

He jabbed hard and fast at my face only to find air. I was behind him already. Using the handle of my knife, I knocked him hard on the head. He dropped like a stone.

Amateur hour.

The rest of the trial went about the same until just a handful of Community members remained, and no humans stood. I'd done my best to avoid kills, but judging by the amount of blood pooling beneath bodies, I might have been alone in that.

Even though I could tell supernatural beings from humans, I couldn't tell what kind they were. This handful was likely just human mages who barely registered as being *other*. I wouldn't know for sure unless they used magic or shifted, but at least I wasn't the only one who couldn't use magic to win.

Hot damn, I missed my paralyzing poisons right about now.

Sweat marked my forehead. The humidity was worse after last night's storm, and I really wished I could turn off my sense of smell. Repeated fights in the arena without bringing in fresh sand and letting it bake under the hot summer sun created an almost unbearable stench.

Three Community members dashed toward me. I let the woman get close before hitting her with an uppercut, her nose cracking. She fell back with her hands at her bloody face.

I pushed her falling body to the side and punched forward again, this time with my knife. The steel bit through a man's abdomen.

He grunted but didn't stop. His spiked mace flew toward me. I ducked, using my momentum to kick my foot up and connect with the side of his head. He stumbled, and I took that second to swing my elbow back at the other guy coming up behind me. His head snapped back, spit flying. I swept his legs out from under him.

Few Community members trained as I did, with weapons and armor and little to no magic. Their inability to function without it was a significant advantage for me.

Deep snarling snagged my attention to the left and raised the hairs on the back of my neck. The last guy had shifted into his wolf form. He leaped, and his massive body slammed me to the ground. My head smacked the arena floor hard, and my vision went swirly.

His teeth descended on my face, and I raised my arm, holding him at bay with my vambrace. I fought to steady my vision. Working my knees up under his belly, I shoved as hard as I could. The force was enough to knock most of his weight off me, and I scrambled away on my hands and knees.

Teeth clamped onto and pierced through my ankle. He tugged hard, and I fell on my stomach. I screamed as my bones crunched between his jaws. Sudden fear laced through me, stealing my breath.

If the others joined in, I'd lose.

I would *not* lose.

My fingernails raked through the sand as I struggled to find a purchase to get back on my feet. A sharp pain shot down one finger, which I was pretty sure meant I'd lost an entire fingernail.

I ground my teeth together and flipped onto my back to face the wolf. Calling on my inner fire, I infused my limbs with added strength. I kicked my free leg out with all my might.

The wolf's snout collapsed in on itself, audibly breaking the bones. The inhuman squeal that came next brought goosebumps all along my body, but he finally let go.

Without another thought, I snatched a knife from my belt and lunged forward on my knees. The blade sank deep into the wolf's eye, and he collapsed.

Sadness swept over me unexpectedly.

Killing vampires didn't really faze me. They'd already died once, and I considered the whole idea of dying for immortality incredibly selfish. Sure, there might be medical reasons for some, but that was the minority. Maybe even rare.

But killing another Community member, a kind that was already pretty damn close to immortal, tugged at my heart. Wolves were usually loyal and noble, fierce and straightforward.

Why had this one wanted to become a bloodsucker?

The only answer I could understand was being cast out of his pack and not dealing well with the shame. He would have been ostracized and hunted down like a rabid dog.

Piercing, burning pain exploded across my body. Ice shot down my arms and legs, freezing me in place.

Someone was using magic.

My eyes still moved, and I strained them to the side to see the king and queen. This was a disqualification. They needed to end the trial and kick this shithead mage into a grave to rot.

Vincenzo and Bianca didn't move. The king sat expressionless, stroking his beard. The queen's hands gripped the arms of her outdoor throne. Her eyes blazed wildly. The crazy bitch was excited to see me die.

Running footsteps and a battle cry behind me told me I was on my own and about to die.

Not today.

I drove a raging inferno out of my body. The ice cracked, and hungry flames flung still frozen shards in all directions. Unleashing my fiery wings, I spun on my knees, raising Lisa just in time to block the killing blow.

The mage stumbled back with a raised arm, away from my flaming body.

The gong boomed, ending the trial.

My body shook from adrenaline and exhaustion. That had been way too close for comfort—twice. I doused my flames but kept my wings out in case anyone tried to do something stupid.

I turned a fuming glare on the king. "What the fuck, man? You should have called it earlier. That was a disqualification."

Angry red sparks flashed in Vincenzo's gaze. I guess he didn't get called out like that often.

"You're both disqualified," Bianca said, her high-pitched voice somehow going up an octave. Her nails dug into the chair's arms, splintering the wood. Blood dripped down the legs.

I jerked my head back in shock. "Excuse me?" I pointed my knife at the sniveling mage who'd dropped to his knees, begging for mercy. "This idiot used magic on me."

"And you also used yours." Her eyes were opened wide, and her exposed skin was flushed pink. She grinned, her fangs extending. "Therefore, you both forfeit the trial. You are ours."

This chick was seriously unhinged.

Beside her, Emilia smiled beneath lowered eyelids. She watched me like a cat watched a mouse. Patient and cunning.

She was Death incarnate.

The blood drained from my face, and my knife quivered in my cold grip.

They couldn't be serious. I hadn't used my magic as a weapon; I used it defensively. Freeing myself from the mage's magical hold. That couldn't possibly be against the rules.

Did they expect me to just be okay dying while I waited for them to consider disqualification instead?

The vampire crowd went wild. Their yells drowned out Bianca's hysterical laughter, and shouts rang out.

Through my haze of disbelief, I realized they weren't cheering for my death.

They were angry…

With their queen.

The king raised his hands for silence. When the crowd settled, he considered me with narrowed eyes. "It appears you've won over the crowd. They would like you to continue to the final trial."

I held my breath. My heart seemed to stop beating.

"We will allow it."

Oh, Sweet Mokosh.

Swallowing hard, I dropped my gaze to the sand. My breaths came out harsh and unsteady. I didn't know how I was still standing. Everything felt numb and tingly.

Above me, Bianca's shrieks faded away, and the crowd continued their deafening cheer.

At some point, the werewolf's body had returned to his human form, naked and faceless. I'd seen some fucked up bodies before, but this was something else. The warm stench of way too much old blood and sweat hit my nose.

I turned to the side and threw up.

CHAPTER 24

Sunday Afternoon

I paced the length of the holding room. Tonight would be the final trial. Just a few more hours until my last obstacle to saving Thane was gone.

Whoever they sent to fight me would try anything to win, including cheat like only vampires could. There were bound to be more loopholes, and I didn't doubt the queen would give my opponent every advantage possible.

The night before, after explaining to the others what had happened during the third trial, I'd left them yelling for justice and passed out on my cot. Bloody, sweaty clothes and all.

I had smelled positively delightful that morning.

"I don't understand why a werewolf would want to become a vampire," I said, unable to get the wolf out of my head. It was also better than focusing on the veritable shitshow that third fight had been.

I winced as I tweaked my injured ankle on a turn. My genetics allowed me to heal at an insanely fast rate, but even broken bones from a werewolf's jaws took time to fully recover.

Annoyance flickered through me. Whatever I faced in the arena later that night, this pain would be a massive hindrance. The good news was this time, I had more than enough magic to burn any infection or wolf-shifting virus out.

Keeping my focus on the wolf also kept my thoughts off Thane. Jessa had called earlier just to say there was no news. He was resting, and the angels were doing everything they could to slow his death.

In this situation, no news was good news.

I had forbidden the others from telling Jessa what had happened during the fight. Nothing would keep me from winning that dragonstone. Once I had it in hand—

No, once we used it and Thane was whole again, *then* I would worry about bringing the vampires to their knees.

"What the hell happened to that wolf?" I asked, wincing once again as my ankle throbbed.

"That was totally out of the blue, and I have no idea," Kit-Angela said. "But I do have something for that pain," She pulled her duffel bag from under the cot and dug through it.

The vampire attendant raised a hand. "No magic is permit—"

"Oh, pipe down," Kit-Angela snapped. She had taken the third fight especially hard. "It's an herbal poultice. Totally natural."

My eyes widened. "It's not that stuff from after the manticore, is it?"

She approached me with the familiar-looking jar. "It is, and you're going to use it. Sit." She unscrewed the lid, releasing the vomit-like smell.

My stomach turned over, but I obeyed her command. She sat beside me.

Walking back in from the bathroom, Lena pinched her nose and waved a hand in front of her face. "Did someone shit their pants? I wasn't even in there for that long."

From his seat on his cot, Ivan laughed through the cloth he held over his nose and mouth. Smart man.

Kit-Angela ignored them both and globbed the poultice on my ankle, rubbing it into my skin. I grimaced and gripped the sheets in my hands as fresh pain shot through my foot and calf.

"You are such a baby," she grumbled. "No wonder you almost…" her voice trailed off.

"What?" I asked through clenched teeth. I glanced down at her hand where she was staring. My stomach clenched, though not from the smell this time.

Oh, fuck.

Angela's pale white hand was turning brown. The disguise was failing.

"Ivan, toss me a towel, would you? This is messy." I lowered my eyelids and glanced at the vampire through my lashes.

He hadn't noticed the lull in our conversation…

Yet.

I grabbed the thrown towel from the air and placed it over my ankle and Kit-Angela's hand.

She wrapped it around the affected skin before raising her gaze to meet mine. Fear shone through her brown eyes. Kit's brown hue, not Angela's.

I turned to the vampire attendant and flashed a strained smile. "Can we have a few minutes of privacy so I can change?"

It wasn't a totally abnormal request, though he'd definitely seen a significant amount of my skin already. He bowed and backed out the door.

"What's up?" Lena approached the cot, eyeing my clothes. "I thought you were wearing that."

Kit unwrapped the towel and showed them her hand. "I'm not sure how much longer it'll last. These spells tend to fade rapidly once they reach their limit."

"You need to go home," I urged.

As much as I wanted her there to see it through with me, I wanted her alive more. If Vincenzo and Bianca found out she'd come back, she'd be a dead witch. I'd be dead, too, for bringing her.

"Even if I wanted to, I can't until this is over," she said, wrapping her hand again. "No one can. You'd be disqualified, for real this time."

There were those pesky rules again, working against me every step of the way.

"Okay, then we need to hide you, tell them you're sick or something."

She gave me a skeptical look. All traces of fear were gone. "You think this is my first time dealing with a failed spell and certain death? I'll be fine. You just worry about the next fight. They don't want you to win, and they're going to do everything they can to make sure you lose."

Ivan and Lena exchanged a nervous glance. I knew what they were thinking. They'd try to protect Kit if the worst happened, and they worried what the vampires might do to *me* thanks to my friends' actions.

Basically, we'd all be screwed.

A knock silenced any further conversation. The vampire attendant opened the door. "Before you change, you've been permitted a shower to look your best at the next trial. If you'll follow me?"

My mouth dropped open. Dreams really did come true.

〜〰〜

A few hours later, I stood at the doors leading into the arena and picked at a thread dangling from my tunic.

This was it. The final fight. If I won, it would be home to Thane forever.

If not…

Well, I wouldn't let myself worry about that last part.

The shower had been ridiculously amazing. The water ran a nasty brownish red through several scrubs, but it turned clear eventually. Steam had done wonders for my sore muscles and hurt ankle. I preferred to give credit to the shower over the poultice so Kit couldn't lord it over my head and try to use it again.

Regardless, I was all sparkly clean and ready to get dirty again. At least the king and queen would be able to properly show off their assumed prize. I was almost sorry to ruin their moment by winning.

High-heels tapped against the floor behind me.

Not expecting anyone, I frowned and turned around.

"Ah, I'm pleased you took me up on my offer, little bird," Emilia said, looking me up and down with an appreciative gaze.

Her crimson dress swished as she approached. The silk fabric did little to hide her curves or milky-white skin.

If she was here to play games again, I'd introduce her to Lisa real fast.

I raised an eyebrow. "What offer?"

"The shower, of course."

Oh. Well, I would always accept a shower, no matter who offered it. "You prefer us strutting like peacocks when we fight?"

Her laugh echoed in the hallway. "Not unless you're hiding a cock under that armor."

I blinked at her.

"Strutting peacocks are male. Peahens are the females." She waved a hand dismissively. "It's a common mistake. I'll make sure you get a proper education during your training." Her hot gaze swept over me again. "You are anything but common."

I rolled my eyes, ignoring the slight tickle in my belly. That wasn't her *influence*—it was a memory of the incredible orgasm she'd almost given me in front of thousands of vampires.

"Don't hold your breath waiting."

She smiled, though it was much more sinister than I expected. "You will lose tonight. I've made sure of it."

My blood chilled to ice. "Excuse me?"

"You think you've eradicated the threat by culling the necromancers," she said with a tsk. "You're delightfully naive."

My thoughts drifted back to the letter I'd received. She had also called me little bird tonight. It had to be her. "Did you send me a letter?"

Her eyebrows pinched together. "What? Don't be stupid. The necromancers were only meant as a distraction."

The gong thundered three times overhead.

"So much to say, so little time," she continued, clasping her hands together. "Just know that I'll enjoy using you to bring down the agency. Galina was so easy to convince all those decades ago. She leaped at the chance of abandoning those stuck-up angels and ruling her own realm. I just hadn't expected you to kill her before she could fulfill her end of the bargain."

My mouth opened, but no words would come out. I didn't know what to say. I wasn't sure I would ever be prepared to hear those words coming from her. Coming from anyone. It should have been over.

Emilia was behind everything this whole time?

Why in Dazhbog's name did she want to bring down the agency?

"And William. Poor, stupid winter fae." She sighed dramatically. "He got too big for his britches, didn't he? All that cold weather must have frozen his brain cells. Thank you for taking care of him for me."

My brain had shut down, malfunctioned. Maybe melted. I could not process what she was saying to me.

How was any of this even possible?

The final gong sounded, and the doors opened.

"Don't worry, little bird, I'll fill you in on all the juicy details after you lose. Don't give up too easily. You know we love a good show." She fluttered her fingers in a dainty wave.

A vampire came around the door and pulled me toward the arena.

"Wait!" I shouted, finally finding my voice. Stumbling in the sand from the unexpected force, I whirled back to face Emilia.

The doors slammed shut, and the lock snapped into place.

What the fucking fuck had just happened?

CHAPTER 25

Sunday Night

Every inch of me was on fire. Not literally, of course, because then I'd lose the trials for cheating. But the unexpected influx of emotions charged my skin with electricity and hummed along my limbs. Goosebumps rose all across my body.

I thought I'd avenged my family by killing Galina. I thought it was all over, and this was the final battle I'd have to face before getting my very happy ending.

How had I been so wrong? So blind?

I racked my brain trying to put the pieces together.

Emilia had only become a Master within the last century. When Xavier was arrested, she had received a massive promotion, moving to Miami from Gainesville. Adam and the agency had been nothing but professional to her, considering her predecessor's betrayal of the Community.

But this plan went even farther back than Xavier. She had convinced Galina to conspire against the agency thirty some odd years ago.

For what?

What could she possibly gain from this?

"We've come to the final trial," Vincenzo's voice rang out over the stadium, demanding attention. "The phoenix has certainly risen to the challenge, but tonight she will face one of our best. A Master who has gone undefeated for centuries."

As the king restated rules that I'd already heard three times, I glanced at my opponent, and my mouth ran dry.

Gabriel, the one I'd dubbed Nightmare in the cemetery, grinned at me from across the arena. His *influence* might not have been as strong as Xavier's—and nowhere near as overpowering as Emilia's—but going undefeated for so long spoke to his level of expertise in the coliseum.

Not only would he want to win this event and maintain his badass reputation, but we'd also seriously pissed him off by ratting out his graveyard shenanigans to his king.

This would be personal.

I licked my dry lips. I had no idea what to do. If I stopped the trial to accuse Emilia, I might not get the chance to fight for the dragonstone. If they believed me, they could hold off the last trial pending an investigation, which could last years.

We didn't have that kind of time.

But if I didn't say anything, Emilia might escape, and there was a good possibility Gabriel would wipe the arena floor with my face. My chance to find out more about whatever the fuck was going on could be lost forever.

What would Thane do?

Emilia stepped out from the shadows behind the royalty box and took her seat beside Bianca.

Hatred rushed forth from the depths of my soul, roaring and writhing, a monster demanding to be unleashed. It was an all-consuming beast, and my rage wouldn't be sated until her death was mine.

The king lifted his arms, a sign that he was about to start the fight.

I pointed Lisa in Emilia's direction and raised my voice, "You have a traitor in your ranks."

A flurry of activity ran through the crowd—gasps, whispers, and boos. I ignored it all, my focus solely on the traitor.

Vincenzo narrowed his eyes and lowered his arms. "We don't take false accusations lightly."

"Good thing it's not false," I said. "Emilia Delacroix is conspiring behind all of your vampiric backs to bring down the Death Enforcement Agency. She manipulated a rogue grim reaper and fae necromancer to overthrow my parents from the phoenix throne."

I met her gaze, channeling all my fury into my eyes. "I demand the right to face her in this trial. After all, she is a Master Vampiress."

A storm brewed in the king's darkening expression. He turned his head slowly toward Emilia. "For what purpose?"

Her tinkling laugh rang out. When no one joined her,

she put a hand on her chest, her eyes widening. "Oh, you don't actually believe her, do you?"

"Do not toy with a king." Power laced through each of his words, and his eyes promised a gruesome punishment.

As his will overpowered hers, she shrank back into the chair. When she regained her composure, she glared at him and stood. "For what purpose? To rise to our rightful place in this world. Vampires have hidden in the angels' shadows for too long.

"Angels should not protect humans. They need to allow the species to evolve. The best of them will survive our hunts and learn to protect themselves, *without* divine intervention. We are not like the others they govern. We are truly immortal, equal to the gods."

She was mighty full of herself.

I inspected the crowd's reaction. Not one of them moved. In fact, it was eerily quiet as they listened to her speak. How many of her supporters had she brought with her, or was she winning over new recruits right now?

"That's not how things are done," Vincenzo growled, his eyes burning crimson. "You've put us at grave risk, all of us, should the angels find out what you've done. We strip you of your title. You are no longer a Master. Seize her."

"That's not how things are done," she mimicked his Italian accent flawlessly and laughed. "No, Vincenzo, I strip *you*."

Death moved swiftly and silently through the crowd. Those siding with Emilia revealed themselves with sharpened stakes, plunging them into their neighbor's hearts. Clouds of dust rose around the stadium before anyone knew what was happening.

Screams and shrieks rent the night air, and chaos erupted.

I ran to the lowest part of the wall leading to the stadium seating and reached up toward the ledge.

"Where is your reaper protector now, girl?" Gabriel's voice taunted me from behind. "I'm ready to shake in my boots."

Godsdamnit. I did *not* have time to deal with his revenge fantasy.

I spun around and flung a wooden knife at him in one swift move. He batted the blade aside like a fly and grinned again.

The last trial was officially over, which meant I didn't have to hold back. Flames licked their way across my body greedily, building into a raging inferno. I spread my wings and lifted off the ground.

Gabriel's eyes bugged out of his head, and he turned to run.

It was way too easy, but I was ready to kill every single vampire in here. One would have to do for now.

Pointing Lisa at his back, I shot a fiery bolt in his direction.

The lightning-like flame whipped itself around him like a flung chain. By the time his body hit the ground, he was nothing but ash. The sparks fizzled out in the sand. One problem down.

Who was equal to the gods now?

I landed on the ledge of the stadium seating. A stake came at me, and I teetered backward. Beating my wings, I caught my balance and swung Lisa. My blade beheaded the vamp, and I snatched the stake from his disintegrating hand.

Glancing at the royalty box only a hundred feet away, scuffles blocked my view and every path I could take. I'd have to fight my way through to get to the traitor. Fine by me, but she better fucking be there to face me.

Newly ignited rage fueled each step I took, red the only color I saw. I swung and chopped, kicked and ducked, taking down anyone who stepped in my way. I didn't care about who was on what side right now.

A vampire was a fucking vampire.

Stepping through another cloud of dust, I stopped short. A head rolled toward me and bumped against my boots.

Vincenzo's dark eyes stared up at me.

His body collapsed, revealing Emilia on the other side. She held a bloodied chain whip between her hands, and Bianca was nowhere to be seen.

Emilia dangled the whip in front of her. "I'll be sure to blame that one on you."

"People have this funny way of underestimating me," I said, kicking the already crumbling head out of my way. "Until they find themselves caught or dead."

Her eyes flashed with the dangerous glint of a predator. "Lucky for me, I'm already dead."

"I've never actually considered your kind to be lucky." I nodded at her whip. "You know chain whips are basically useless as a weapon, right?"

"Tell that to Vincenzo." She drew the whip up into the air and cracked it in my direction. The serrated steel edges shot toward me.

I leaped onto the nearest seat, jumped into the air, and shifted into falcon form. Diving for her, I stretched out my talons and slashed them across her face. I was gone before she raised her whip again.

She growled as I soared above her. The bloody gashes marking her cheeks and nose were already healing.

I swooped in close to taunt her, trilling in amusement when her whip went sailing by.

"You're no match for me," she called up. She tossed the whip aside and grabbed a fallen sword. "I've been training and fighting for centuries before you were born. I've outwitted you every step of the way."

It seemed like her parents taught her the importance of positive self-talk, too.

I landed nearby and shifted back to my human form, Lisa still in hand. "I admit you had me fooled; you had all of us fooled. But I guarantee I'm going to kick your ass straight back to the grave."

Only metaphorically, of course, since she'd simply disintegrate. But I liked the way it sounded.

She came at me. After a few passes testing each other, I had to admit she was pretty damn good with a sword. But better than I was? That was still to be seen.

I could easily set myself on fire or send a spark her way to speed things up, but I wanted to know who was truly superior. Vanity was calling, and I answered.

Plus, if she was brighter than I wanted to give her credit for, she likely invested in flame retardant clothing after hearing about my encounter with Xavier.

Not that I'd managed to set him on fire, but I had certainly tried.

The more we sparred, the more I appreciated the challenge she presented. She moved like a dancer, graceful and elegant. Her full red lips parted the longer we fought, and a light sheen covered her forehead and chest.

A bead of sweat slipped from her collarbone and dipped between her breasts. I bit my lip as a deep ache pulsed between my legs. I wanted to follow that drop with my tongue, lick the sweat down to her perfect breasts.

I blocked her next strike and frowned. Hesitation kept me from following up with a counterattack, even though an easy opening appeared. I didn't want to fight her.

I wanted to make her scream…

In pleasure.

Somewhere in the back of my mind, panic reared its head.

Stumbling back a step, I shook my head, trying to clear my muddled thoughts.

"What's the matter, little bird?" she cooed.

I blinked in confusion and lowered my blade. Why was I attacking her?

Her very kissable lips pulled up into a smirk, and she crooked a finger at me, calling me to her.

Yes, I would do anything for her. I took a step forward.

A sharp pain stabbed through the left side of my chest, through my heart. I cried out and doubled over, pressing a hand to the wound.

Except, nothing had hit me.

I pulled down my top enough to see an angry red mark pulsating on my skin—a falcon in flight.

Thane.

With a shuddering gasp, I regained control of my senses.

For fuck's sake. Emilia and her godsdamn *influence* again. No one could deny she was hot, but that didn't mean I wanted to sleep with the undead vegetable. She could go rot in her garden for all I cared.

I burned the rest of her temptation out of my head and snapped my head up with a snarl.

She threw her head back and laughed. "Oh, you are just too easy to play with. We'll have so much fun together, you and I."

Launching myself forward, I attacked without mercy. Again and again, I swung and thrust, jabbed and feinted, relentlessly pushing her back step by step. She defended each blow with a smile on her face, a smile I wanted to obliterate.

This was no longer about being the best.

I would end her no matter how dirty I had to fight. Nothing would bring me more satisfaction right now than sending her head flying and stomping across her ashes.

She had nearly caged me, but I was no one's pet. Xavier had learned that lesson the hard way.

So would she.

An opening appeared, and I thrust again. She blocked my strike at the last moment, and I danced out of reach.

"As much as I've enjoyed our time dancing together, little bird, this is getting tedious." She ran her free hand down the length of her sword. Flames followed her touch, rushing down the blade.

Ognebog's balls, that was phoenix fire. Icy dread swept through my veins and clutched at my throat. I should have known Galina would share that secret with others. Few knew the only way to kill a phoenix—as in no resurrecting— was with her own fire.

"I can tell by that look on your face you know what this is." She jabbed at me, taunting. "Galina sent me a gift."

That name thawed the ice gripping me.

"You can't even beat me without using my own magic." Deflecting her blade, I shook my head and tsked. "Pathetic, really."

Emilia's smile faltered as she circled me. "You have been nothing but a problem since the day we met. A thorn I'm going to enjoy plucking from my side."

"I am a problem that you will learn to regret." My voice was even and calm despite the fury and fear coursing through my limbs. Both emotions wanted a piece of her, and I was ready to feed them. I pulled a stake from my belt behind my back.

Blocking her next swing with Lisa, I held her arm above our heads and plunged the stake into her open side.

Her eyes opening wide, she looked down at the stake and gave a short, incredulous laugh. "Your aim is terrible, little bird."

I waited until she met my gaze again. "Wood burns, sweetheart."

With a snap of my fingers—mostly for effect, of course—the stake burst into flames, a hungry blaze licking its way through her insides.

She screamed as she stumbled backward and dropped her sword. Grabbing at the stake, she wrenched it free from her side.

Except my fire had already claimed its prize, engulfing her in a ravenous inferno. Thick black smoke rose from her disintegrating figure, and her dress fell to the ground, mostly unscathed.

Oh look, I was right.

It *was* flame retardant.

Thane

Every part of me hurt. I had refused all medications the angels offered. I'd died on drugs once already. I wasn't going to do it again.

Taking a deep breath, I immediately wished I hadn't. Another cough overwhelmed my frail, dying body. My diaphragm spasmed with each harsh sound, leaving me breathless and wheezing.

When it finally subsided, I kept my eyes closed, too tired to open them.

Lord, send me strength because I am pathetic.

At least Veronica was worth it.

Someone leaned over my hospital bed to change out the cold cloth across my forehead.

"You should really let me ease your pain," said Jessa's sweet voice.

Swallowing hurt, but I accepted the cool water she brought to my lips. I didn't know why she bothered anymore, but she refused to listen to me.

"There's no point. It's over," I managed to get out, my voice raspy despite the drink.

"Thane Munro, don't you dare say that again," she scolded and squeezed my hand. "I haven't stayed by your side this whole time just to let you give up on the last night. She'll make it in time."

I wished I believed her.

For the second time tonight, my heart seized with intense pain, and my back arched off the bed.

Jessa ran to the door and yelled something I couldn't hear over the wildly beeping machines. Her blue-green eyes appeared over me, filled with fear and sorrow.

"Thane!" she yelled, shaking my shoulders. "Don't you dare give up on her!"

I wanted to laugh at the absurdity of her demand. Give up on Veronica? Never. Of course she would win; she was too stubborn not to. I had just run out of time.

The monitor's beeping flatlined, and I exhaled for the last time.

She loved me, and I loved her. That's all that mattered.

I would give my life for her any day.

CHAPTER 26

Sunday Night

The vampires who had been closing in on my fight with Emilia were next. I flicked my fingers, sending a spark jumping from the already dying blaze that had once been the Master Vampiress. It snagged on the nearest undead creature.

He screamed and flailed his arms, somehow thinking that would help his situation. Except he ended up setting his friends on fire. The flames reached out and grabbed anyone nearby, overwhelming and ravaging the remaining vampire population that hadn't been wise enough to flee.

Unfortunately, there weren't that many of the bloodsuckers left.

"Veronica!" Ivan's shout drew my attention behind the royal viewing box to the inner workings of the coliseum where he stood with Lena and Kit.

I strode through the flames that were devastating the expensive furniture set up for royalty, the heat nothing but a gentle caress against my skin. No other vampires attacked me, a fact I was almost sad about.

Right now, I wanted to kill them all.

When I reached my friends, I did a double-take. Kit's skin had turned a mottled pattern of brown and white, and one shoulder was a few inches higher than the other. The hunchback of Miami had arrived.

"Oh, dear gods, is that as painful as it looks?" I asked, unable to keep the horror out of my voice.

She glared at me just as her lower shoulder popped up, ruining the effect of her new look. She sighed. "No, just mildly inconvenient. Let's go get that fucking rock and get the hell out of here."

"Warn us next time you start a brawl, will you?" Ivan grinned as we ran down the curving stone corridor.

"I'll do my best," I said with a matching grin. We passed multiple openings leading back into the arena. Smoke billowed up into the dark sky. "Do we even know where the stone is?"

We slowed as we approached a closed wooden door at the end of the hall.

"Lucky for you, I do." Kit pointed at the door. "The magic within it shares common traits with elemental magic."

"How does that help?" Lena asked. She opened the door slightly to peek through, her sword held ready.

"It acts like a homing beacon to my kind," Kit explained.

Lena nodded and slipped through the opening. The rest of us followed, and Kit took the lead. A few more doors down, the corridor swung abruptly to the left, away from the arena.

Around the corner, a brood of vampires guarded the last door, which was cracked open. This one was made entirely from thick steel that looked like it could withstand a hurricane or a bomb. A keypad sat where a keyhole would typically be, and a contraption like a steel ship's wheel took up the middle.

Ivan winked out of existence only to appear in the vampires' midst. He set himself on fire and reached out to touch those closest to him before they even realized he was there. The flames grew fast as they devoured clothing and skin.

Lena shifted forms and launched herself toward the ceiling. She swooped close to the guards and dove, changing back to her human form mid-air. Her sword shredded through them like paper before her feet touched the ground.

Kit whistled. "Damn. Don't ever let me get into a brawl with those two."

I grinned, feeling immense pride for my best friend's approval of my newest friends. When the last vamp fell in a cloud of dust, we strode to the door, leaving our footprints in the ash.

Lena pulled the door open farther, peeked through, then swung it open the rest of the way.

The room inside was hardly more than a decent-sized walk-in closet in a middle-class home, except surrounded by steel walls, floor, and ceiling like a panic room. Metal shelves filled with trinkets and weapons were affixed to each wall.

An empty pedestal stood in the center. Beside it was Bianca.

The queen's face whirled toward us, a wild snarl on her lips. Bloody tears streaked her once beautiful face. In her hands, she held a rock.

A rock that I desperately needed.

"You have brought nothing but chaos and ruin with you," she spat at me. "You destroyed a millennia-old tradition. You don't deserve this." Her face crumbled. "Vincenzo is gone because of you."

I stared at her in shock, not sure if I was hearing her correctly. Did this creature actually care about her husband's death?

She wiped at her face and glared at me. "Oh, we can see what you're thinking. You believe our kind to be incapable of love. That just shows how stupid you really are."

I raised my empty hands. "I won't disagree about all that, but I'm not leaving without that stone. I need to save the man *I* love."

New red drops spilled down her cheeks. "It won't work."

"I really don't want to kill you right now." *Lie.* "But I'm taking that stone one way or another."

"Kill me if you wish, but the stone doesn't work."

Her words sank like bricks in my stomach. "What do you mean?"

"I tried to use it on Fortunato." She sniffled, pointing toward a shelf. The heart box stood open, covered in bloody fingerprints. "You can see how well that worked."

Plenty of reasons for the failed resurrection rolled through my mind, like the fact that he was already dead long before he became nothing but a beating heart. A different kind of dead than Thane, who still possessed a whole body. I didn't think she would want to hear any of that right now, though.

I held out my hand. "I have to try."

Her tears dried as quickly as they'd come, and her expression hardened. "No."

The bonding mark burned red hot. I yelped and pressed a hand to my chest.

Ivan was at my side in a flash, his eyes glowing. "What happened? Did she hurt you?"

I shook my head and pulled my top down enough to see it. The falcon-shaped mark pulsed once more with incredible heat, then faded to a dull red. I'd never seen it that color before. It was almost…

Lifeless.

I touched it. My skin beneath the image was cool to the touch for the first time.

Terror like I'd never known before seized me, and I gasped for breath.

Was I too late?

Ivan took my hand and turned to Lena and Kit. "I'll be back for you soon."

Understanding filled Lena's gaze, and she nodded.

My vision went so black, I thought I'd passed out. Except a second later, we were standing right next to Bianca.

She flinched back and turned to flee.

Ivan grabbed her arm with his free hand, and the world disappeared.

As we popped back into existence, Bianca shrieked.

Behind the desk in front of us, a woman jumped in her seat, spilling steaming coffee across her lap. She yelped and leaped to her feet.

I recognized her. We were outside the hospital wing of the DEA in Miami.

Ignoring Bianca's continued shrieking, I grabbed the vampire and dragged her through the double doors. Angels and reapers in blue scrubs came running, but I pushed past them and continued down the brightly lit hall. I would have to apologize for the ruckus later.

We were almost there.

"Shut up!" I yelled and gave Bianca's arm a yank. She finally stopped screaming, but she cringed from all the light. "It's not even as bad as the reapers' way of teleportation."

The mark on my chest cooled even more. My lungs constricted, stealing my breath. A chill sank deep into my bones, and my eyes stung.

Two more doors. Just two more. So close.

I was going to make it.

Adam stepped out of Thane's room, pressing his lips together in a thin line. He caught sight of me barreling down the hall, a crazed vamp with a bloodied face on my heels, and held up his hands for me to stop. His expression was enough to make my knees buckle, and he caught me as I started to fall.

"I am truly sorry, Ms. Neill," he said.

No. This wasn't happening. I made it back alive, victorious. I had the dragonstone. This was going to work.

I regained my balance and brushed past him, hauling Bianca along behind me.

My heart stopped as I entered the room.

Everything stopped.

Thane lay on the same bed in which I'd left him, IVs and other devices still attached to his body. His face was calm, at peace. The heart rate monitor flashed with lights, but no sound came out.

It wouldn't have mattered—there was no mistaking the flat line's meaning.

I spun toward Bianca and closed in until our noses almost touched. Through gritted teeth, I spat out each word, "Give. Me. The. Stone."

Whatever she saw in my face must have been convincing. She slipped the rock into my hand, and I ran to Thane's side.

Except… I didn't know what to do.

The stone was made for my kind. A gift for a queen. Instinct would know what to do. I was sure of it.

I took a deep breath and placed the rock on the middle of his chest. Nothing happened. I covered it with my hand and pushed magic into it, urging it to work.

Still nothing.

"Adam!" I yelled over my shoulder. "How do I make this thing work?"

The archangel entered the room. His wings drooped behind him, and his bright blue eyes sparkled with tears. "I do not know."

"You said it's supposed to be able to cure death." Panic rose within me, making it hard to breathe.

My grip tightened on the stone. Was this thing even the dragonstone? Had we all been fooled?

Was this entire ordeal for nothing?

"It appears that may have just been a rumor. Or we are simply too late."

No.

I refused to believe that. Despite the monitor's flat line, I checked his neck for a pulse. For the first time since we'd met, his skin was cool to the touch, just like my mark had been. No pulse beat beneath my fingers.

I pinched his nose and tilted his head back, breathing into his open mouth. I climbed onto the bed, straddled him, and used both hands to press into his chest. Again and again, I pumped for his heart and breathed for his lungs, willing his body to do the rest. To start again.

My breaths grew raspy and short, my hands clammy. I refused to believe this was the end. Tears clouded my vision as I counted each push against his chest.

"Veronica, stop," Kit's calm voice was at my side. Ivan must have gone to bring them back already. She placed her hand on my arm. "He's gone, babe."

A sob erupted from my throat, and I collapsed onto his chest. My body shook with each sob. The rock dug into my cheek, but I didn't care. The tears continued to flow, and I wasn't sure they would ever stop.

I had lost Thane. I had lost the love of my life, my literal soulmate.

An orange glow appeared behind my closed eyelids.

I sat up fast, blinking and wiping my face. The rock's center was glowing, pulsing with an orangish-yellow light. It was wet with my tears. Steam drifted off the stone as the colors continued to brighten, dazzling in their intensity.

My eyes widened as a swirling yellow strand of magic rose from the dragonstone. The thread drifted toward

Thane's face and slipped into his open mouth. Beneath his skin, his throat glowed, and more of the magic pulled from the stone to fill his body.

As the strand continued to unravel, the dragonstone grew smaller on his chest until it was simply gone. The last of the thread disappeared between his lips.

Silence filled the room.

A beat appeared in the monitor's flat line. Then another. Thane gasped, drawing in a breath like a drowning man.

The mark on my chest ignited like a fresh brand. An exquisite feeling of pain and pleasure that I welcomed.

His eyes flew open, and his beautiful ocean-blue gaze settled on me, still straddling his hips. His lips twisted into that delicious smirk.

"Well, I'd die any day to wake up to this sight."

CHAPTER 27

Sunday Night

My squeal of joy probably shattered some eardrums. It worked! Holy shit, it had worked.

I threw myself across Thane's chest with a little more gusto than the last time. Every inch of my body was electrified with his touch.

He grunted beneath me. "I may be healed, but I can still feel pain."

"I don't care. Shut up," I murmured, nuzzling into his warm neck. He smelled like a perfect mixture of sweet and spicy, of salty ocean breezes. He smelled like home. "I thought I lost you."

"Not going to happen. Don't you know better than that

by now?" He wrapped his arms around my waist, holding me to him. He sniffed. "You reek."

I laughed. He smelled delightful, and I smelled like dozens of vampire carcasses. Whatever I smelled like now, it wasn't half as bad as before my shower. He got lucky.

"That makes too much sense," Kit muttered beside me.

I had almost forgotten anyone else was in the room witnessing this miracle.

Sniffling, I turned my head enough to look at her while still snuggled into Thane. "What does?"

"The dragons created the stone from their tears," she explained. "It took tears to use it."

In all the mystery and chaos involved in finding the dragonstone, I hadn't even thought to ask how to use it. I had assumed it would just... work. Which sounded ridiculously dumb now, but I was in good company.

No one else had asked either.

I slipped the rest of my body to Thane's side, allowing the others to see him. I wasn't willing to stop touching him just yet. His fingers entwined with mine, and he stroked my palm with his thumb.

Despite the constant influx of visitors, Thane's gaze constantly returned to mine. Desire burned within those depths, ravenous to feel alive in the most intimate way.

It dawned on me then that he was truly alive, and not just reaper alive. He wasn't a reaper anymore. He was just...

Thane Munro. My soulmate.

"Give us the room," he said finally, his voice gruff and demanding. His gaze never left mine, and the intensity there threatened to devour me whole.

My core clenched with sudden need, and butterflies

danced in my stomach.

The others chuckled knowingly but listened all the same. Lena even reached over and closed the blinds. What a doll.

When the door clicked shut, Thane shifted toward me. His mouth descended on mine hungrily, a starving man stumbling upon a feast. Reaching behind my neck, he held me firmly in place as his lips claimed mine. His tongue darted between my teeth. Seeking, loving, needing.

His other hand moved down my chest, squeezing my breast through the thick tunic. I gasped into his mouth and pushed my chest towards him, wanting more.

"What is with…" he growled between kisses, "these tunics?"

"Lena will kill me if we ruin another one." Chuckling, I pushed his hand away before he could rip it like he did before. I rolled off the bed.

Leaning forward, he pulled his hospital gown up and over his head. It landed by the door.

As I slowly undid my tunic's ties, his deep blue gaze drank me in. I let the fabric hang loose, playing peekaboo with the curves of my breasts and waist as I pushed my pants to the floor. I let the tunic fall from my shoulders.

The sheet covering his lower half rose with his straining erection.

"My God, you're beautiful," he breathed.

I climbed back onto the bed and pulled the blanket down, freeing his eager length. Straddling his hips again, I leaned forward and kissed his mouth, biting and sucking on his lower lip. I reached between us to grasp his rock-hard cock and guided him toward my opening. I needed him inside me.

He groaned against my lips as I stroked his tip up and down my slit. His hands gripped my hips and squeezed, moving me into the position he wanted. With one thrust, he sheathed himself inside me fully.

"Oh, yes!" I cried out, each stroke sending fire through my core. I sat up and put my hands on his chest. Rolling my hips, I matched his rhythm, loving each thrust as he filled me.

His hand moved up from my hip to cup a breast, rolling my nipple between his fingers.

Shocks radiated outward from his touch, and I dug my nails into his chest, trying to relieve some of the tension building within me.

His gaze seared into mine, powerful and hungry, and his other hand dipped between my legs. He rubbed my clit, sending me into a frenzy.

My eyelids fluttered shut as I moaned. I worked my hips harder against him, the need to release building with every thrust. The flame inside of me grew to an impossible heat, burning me from within. Not painfully, but yearning for more.

"Oh, yes, Thane," I moaned again. "Harder. Fuck me harder."

His hands moved back to my hips as he pounded into me, giving me what I wanted.

The orgasm took me hard. My back bent backward, my world shattering with unbridled pleasure. Heat consumed me, obliterated me from the inside out.

His fingers digging into my skin, Thane groaned as he released.

I collapsed onto him, my hair clinging to my sweaty face. "Wow."

Deep chuckles rumbled through his chest. "I'd say you're welcome, but it was a definite wow for me, too."

Pushing damp hair off my face, I rolled to the side of the small bed. A black line on the far wall caught my eye. I sat up quickly, my mouth dropping open.

A ring of black char circled the entire room. Paint peeled at the edges of the burn. One picture frame lay shattered on the floor, the other hung crooked on the wall, holding on for dear life.

"Oh, shit."

Thane tucked his hands behind his head, a smug look crossing his face. "I made you explode. Quite literally."

Covering my face with my hands, I fell back onto the bed and laughed. "Oh, sweet Mokosh. I've got to get that under control before I burn a whole building down."

"You better not get it under control."

I raised an eyebrow at him. "You like making me explode, huh?" I trailed a hand up his naked thigh. His body responded eagerly to the touch, ready for more. "Do you also like it when I moan your name?"

With a growl that sent shivers of desire racing through me, he rolled on top of me, pinning me to the bed. Both his hands clasped mine and held them above my head. His dark, hungry gaze roved over my naked body as he spread my thighs with his knee.

"I want you to scream it."

CHAPTER 28

Friday Afternoon

Thane interlaced his fingers with mine as we strolled down the beach. In our free hands, we carried our flip-flops, and sand squished beneath our bare feet. Seagulls cawed overhead, passing by or diving toward the low waves for a snack. The sun drifted lazily toward the western horizon, and shadows grew longer with each minute.

Almost a week had passed since I thought I'd lost Thane forever. Within an hour of his waking, the hospital had released him. The angelic staff praised their god's name for his divine miracle.

After a quick discussion with Adam before Thane's release, we had decided to keep the dragonstone's use a secret. While the archangel had more faith in people than I did, he agreed some *eager* Community members might go exploring in dragon lands, searching for more stones.

Not that they could just waltz into Mirognya whenever they wanted. Not without paying a realm walker a hefty sum and facing time in prison if they were caught. I wasn't ready to open a portal just yet, not until we figured out if Emilia's grand plans had shriveled to nothing as she had.

So far, we had no reason to believe that the conspiracy lived, but I also wasn't willing to take any chances yet. We still hadn't figured out who had sent the letter, either.

Adam had enlisted a team of reapers to take Bianca back to Italy and assist in cleanup. He was troubled to hear about my near-disqualification and the queen's refusal to play by her own rules. He'd made it very clear to her that if she attempted to blame me or anyone other than Emilia, he would be forced to step in, using his full authority over the Community.

Thankfully, all the fight had fled from Bianca after that discussion. In true vampiric fashion, she eagerly looked forward to selecting a new king.

Warm ocean breezes teased my hair back from my face and kept the humidity from becoming too stifling. I breathed in the salt-filled air, laced with the hint of bergamot and lavender—Thane's scent. I squeezed his hand.

He turned his face toward me and smiled. His sunglasses kept me from seeing those gorgeous eyes that matched the waves today, but I felt his happiness through our soul link.

That discovery had been a delightful gift accompanying our matching marks. We could feel each other's moods and emotions, becoming stronger the closer we were physically. When combined with his arousal and release, my orgasms had reached nearly catastrophic levels.

Likely sensing my rising desire, he squeezed my hand. I smiled and returned the gesture.

A few days ago, Ivan had returned to Sokol to fill Pietr in on all the happenings. I'd somehow convinced him and Lena that it would be in everyone's best interest if I wasn't around when Pietr got the news about the Blood Trials, even if I did win. Something told me he'd need some time to cool off before facing me.

Lena had stayed with me, convinced I would do something reckless in her absence. I hadn't argued too much—I did have a history, after all. But I had a sneaking suspicion her staying wasn't just about me.

My fierce warrior friend had pestered Kit with more than a few questions about Holly, the witch in Rome. I was sure she would be asking to "go on vacation" any day now.

For now, she flew high above us, keeping watch without interfering.

Kit finally told Angela what really happened in Italy and what I had promised Octavia. As expected, Angela was much more upset about the lie and subsequent distance from her betrothed rather than the actual meeting. I felt terrible for making the situation worse, but Kit made her bed by hiding the truth for so long.

The full moon was only a few days away, which meant my bestie would need to make good on her promise and visit her mom for the first time in decades. Angela demanded to meet her fiancée's mother and probably wanted to keep an eye on her—on *both* of them. Making sure neither woman did anything dumb.

Angela was a keeper for sure.

Kit argued against me joining them, claiming my chaotic nature would somehow make an even bigger mess. Except there was a zero percent chance that I would let her go while her magic was bound. Thankfully, Thane took my side, and I bullied her into submission by threatening a snuggle fest.

Besides, I wanted to snoop around and find out more about the tongueless vampire, Shirley.

Not far in the distance, the Cape Florida Lighthouse stood tall and proud. Sunlight reflected off the white tower and the windows up top, becoming a shining beacon even during the day.

The lighthouse had always been a favorite place to visit in falcon form, and a giddy excitement coursed through me, knowing that I was going to explore it now with my mate.

"I feel like this isn't real life," I said, finally breaking the silence. "How is this real?"

His lips twisted into that delightful smirk I loved so much, and my whole body warmed in response. He was such a beautiful man.

And he was all mine.

"God works in mysterious ways," he said, then laughed as I nudged his arm. "You can't deny a divine intervention in this pairing."

I pulled him to a stop and sat in the warm sand, stretching my legs out before me. Thane sat behind me, pulling me into his chest, and rested his chin on my head.

Happiness like I'd never known enveloped every fiber of my being.

This was heaven.

"I heard you, you know," he said quietly.

I drew my eyebrows together. "When?"

"When you sat by my hospital bed before the trials."

Goosebumps rose on my skin as I remembered the fear coursing through my body that day.

He rubbed my arms, soothing away the bumps and the memories with his warmth. "You said you hadn't asked what I was, what kind of supernatural being."

"Hmm," I murmured, remembering. "So, what are you?"

His chuckle vibrated against his chest. "I'm a realm walker."

I leaned forward to turn and face him, opening my eyes wide. "You have got to be kidding me."

His teeth flashed as he grinned. "Tell me you don't believe in divine intervention now."

Holy fuck.

As a realm walker, he would be able to jump us back and forth from Mirfeniksa—to and from anywhere, anytime we wanted. I didn't need to rely solely on Ivan, as helpful as he had been. I was sure he'd be glad to do his own thing again, anyway.

Realm walkers didn't have the same lifespan as a phoenix, but we would still have a century or two of happiness. I would take it.

I leaned back against him, my soulmate, and he wrapped his arms around me.

Together, we watched as the waves crested and lapped against the sand.

EPILOGUE

Tremors rocked the mountainous caves. The ground rumbled, shaking rocks loose and tumbling across the cavern's expansive floor. With a deafening roar, boulders broke from the cave walls and crashed their way down.

A long, sinuous black neck covered in dust rose from the rubble. The beast shook himself and pushed onto his front legs, legs that hadn't been used in…

How long had it been since he'd last awoken?

All around Imos, others stirred and woke. Chunks of the cave fell to pieces around him. When the last *drakony* broke free of his sleeping place, Imos looked around.

"Who has summoned us from our slumber?" His deep voice was as gravelly as the rocks surrounding him.

A hooded, two-legged figure stepped out of the shadows and onto a ledge, halfway up from the floor. The figure bowed. "Forgive me, Great Imos."

Imos lowered his head to gaze directly into the newcomer's face. His head was at least as tall as the newcomer's entire body. "Speak."

"The dragonstone has been used," it said.

A grumble rolled throughout the cavern as the other dragons expressed their distaste at the news.

"Explain," Imos demanded, straining to keep his anger in check. Waking to such news was not pleasant. They'd had a deal.

"A phoenix who claims to be the new tsarina of Mirfeniksa," the figure said. "She used it on a dying grim reaper. A man she claims is her bonded mate."

This time, the dragons roared with fury, shaking the mountain caves. The two-legged figure stepped back to avoid the falling rocks.

Harsh voices called out in a cacophony of roars:

"A grim reaper?"

"Outrage!"

"Blasphemy!"

"She should be ours!"

Imos spread his massive wings, the tips brushing against the far walls of the cave. "To war!"

The horde of dragons launched themselves into the air, circling upward toward the opening miles above.

Beneath the hood, the figure smiled.

Thanks for reading! I hope you enjoyed the adventure.
*Please consider adding a short review on **Amazon** and/or*
***Goodreads** to let other readers know what you thought.*

I love to get to know my readers. You can reach me on Facebook, Instagram, or Twitter **@stephaniemirro**. Sign up for my mailing list to get new release information, special deals, giveaways, become a part of my ARC team, and more. I look forward to hearing from you!

www.stephaniemirro.com

Veronica's story continues in…

WINGS

OF

DECEIT

THE LAST PHOENIX: BOOK SIX

Coming December 30th.

GLOSSARY

Adam Larue – Archangel of Miami

Adrik – phoenix; rebel leader

Albert Renauldo, Dr. – human plastic surgeon; owns Star Island mansion

Annika – phoenix; high priestess

Anthony "Tony" – piano shop owner; friend of Veronica

Bianca D'Angelo – vampire; Queen of the European Vampire Association

Broderick Ó Faoláin – fae duke; *deceased*

Colin Ó Broin – Autumn Court fae

Charlotte Blanchet – Master Vampiress in the European Vampire Association

Death Enforcement Agency – also known as the DEA;

agency of the human world that keeps the Community safe

Drystan Neill – father of Veronica; *deceased*

El Sombra Mercado – also known as the Shadow Market

Emilia Delacroix – Master Vampiress of Miami

Enrique Alvarez – human street musician

Federico Russo – natural born warlock; *deceased*

Feodora – phoenix; rebel leader

Fortunato – vampire; one of the *veteres*, the originals; *deceased*

Frank Turner – human mage; ex-necromancer

Gabriel – Master Vampire in the European Vampire Association

Galina Volkov – unknown species; false tsarina

Giovanni "Joe" Facchini – fae regular of The Morning Grind; friend of Veronica

Holly – natural born witch; Kit's friend

Isaac Davidson – human manager of The Morning Grind; Veronica's ex-boss

Ivan – phoenix; rebel

Jackson Reed – realm walker; in prison

Jessa – angel; healer

Katherine "Kit" Parker – natural born witch; best friend of Veronica

Katya – phoenix; birdkeeper

Lizabeta "Liz" – phoenix; healer

Luciana Pérez – natural born witch; owner of The Witch's Brew shop in *el Sombra Mercado*

Luka Navarro – alpha of the Miami werewolf pack

Maddox "Mad" Neill – brother of Veronica; *deceased*

Mama Anya – phoenix; midwife

Manuel – owner of food truck in *el Sombra Mercado*

Mila – phoenix; rebel leader

Mirdrakona – dragon lands in Mirognya

Mirfeniksa – phoenix lands in Mirognya

Mirognya – "world of the sun"

Mirvody – merfolk waters in Mirognya

Nathan – angel; fighter

Octavia Parker – natural born witch; Kit's mother

Officer Harris – receptionist at prison; species unknown but most likely a troll

Oleg – phoenix; rebel fire communicator

Owen Cooper, Dr. – head mortician and grim reaper at the DEA

Papa Boris – phoenix

Pavel – phoenix; rebel

Philip – Master Vampire in the European Vampire Association

Pietr – phoenix; rebel leader

Rhiannon Neill – mother of Veronica; *deceased*

Rogelio Diaz – natural born warlock; deep in his cup somewhere

Sophia Clark – grim reaper agent of the DEA

Tabitha Delgado – werewolf

Taisiya – phoenix; rebel leader

Thane Munro – grim reaper agent of the DEA

The Morning Grind – a DC-based coffee shop in Miami; Veronica's day job

Veronica "V" Neill – the last phoenix

Viktor – phoenix; rebel spy

Vincenzo Morella – vampire; King of the European Vampire Association

Vladimir – phoenix; palace guard

Walter Whitmore – human; Octavia Parker's butler

William Caomhánach – Winter Court fae and unseelie

Xavier Garcia – Master Vampire of Miami

Yelena "Lena" – phoenix; rebel

Yury – phoenix; rebel scout

Zasha – phoenix; Veronica's aunt

ACKNOWLEDGEMENTS

First and foremost, thank YOU, my dear reader, for sticking with me and waiting patiently for this book. Publishing took way longer than expected, thanks to an epic (kind of unplanned) vacation, a move to a new state, and overall anxiety. I hope it was everything you hoped it would be.

Secondly, my husband. Though he may not have agreed with all my financial decisions (hee hee), he was still my champion through it all.

Big thanks are also due to my editor, Melissa Simmons; and my beta readers, Marty, Tom, Kimmie, Jessica, Alisha, Rachel, Lauren, and Erica, who made the time for this book despite my disastrously poor timing.

I deeply appreciate Claire Holt's talent, whose covers bring all the readers to my yard. Her work is amazing.

And a loving shout out my friends, family, and fans, who show support in so many ways and motivate me to keep going. Thank you.

I love knowing that my stories make you smile (or cry, muahaha).

ABOUT THE AUTHOR

Stephanie Mirro's lifetime love of ancient mythology led to a college major in the Classics, which wasn't as much fun as writing her own mythology stories. But that education, combined with an overactive imagination and a love for all things fantasy resulted in a writing career.

Although born and raised in Southern Arizona, Stephanie now resides in Georgia with her husband, two kids, and two furbabies. This thing called "seasons" is still magical.

www.ingramcontent.com/pod-product-compliance
Lightning Source LLC
Chambersburg PA
CBHW060920190726
48286CB00002B/573